945 Cedar Avenue

by KC Decker

This is a work of fiction. Names, characters, places, and incidents either are a product of the author's imagination or are used fictitiously. Any resemblance to actual persons; living or dead, businesses, companies, locales, or event is entirely coincidental.

Cover Design by Larch Gallagher
Copyright 2018 By KC DECKER

ISBN-10: 0-9993334-6-1
ISBN-13: 978-0-9993334-6-4

We are all Phoenix
We burn in our sorrows
We rise from it too

—Saru Singhal

Chapter One

Thinking

Damn, that girl has my heart. I cannot think of a more perfect woman than Jessie Hayes. She is *stacked,* and that body torments me constantly. The fact that I've seen her naked on several occasions will be my complete undoing, I'm positive of it.

The first time I saw her perfect tits she was masturbating for her laptop camera. She had been broadcasting her arched back, straining nipples, and spread thighs for that numb nut, Silas. That's when I knew I had to have her, never mind company policy—I'd rather quit and live in poverty for the rest of my life than keep her off limits a second longer. Of course, that's when I told her that I loved her, a tiny detail that upon further reflection, I should have kept to myself.

She didn't tell me she loved me back, and she certainly didn't draw me into her perfect nakedness for the fuck of the century. No, she started crying and shaking her head back and forth—as if the tears weren't soul-annihilating enough. Suffice it to say that was not the reaction I was looking for. But the image of her with her fingers in her panties and her body wrenched back over some pillows—so her tits *flaunted* themselves at me, will be forever etched in my memory. More like burned into my memory, to surface at the most inopportune times imaginable. I can literally not even look at the woman without picturing

1

her topless, and all the things I have done to her in my alone time would shock a high budget porn star.

That little showdown in the hotel room with Jessie and her dime piece of a body had me on the brink of needing to nut under my desk before any sort of a meeting with her. And that lasted for *months*. Her body is only part of the package though. She is really smart, and I have never met anyone with a personality like hers. She's like a dude, in that, she is funny, and you can joke around with her. But she's also deep and tuned in on an emotional level that is just the right amount for me.

She was an extreme emotional support for me after my tours in Baghdad, and she didn't even know ten percent of what I had gone through. She didn't push me like my, now ex-wife had. Jessie made herself a constant, quiet presence that held me up from the inside, like an emotional scaffolding. She knew it was bad, and that I was tormented beyond reason. She would sit with me in my dark house for hours at a time and do nothing but hold my hand. It sounds crazy, but I had drawn strength from her—not enough to function, but enough to go on.

I knew I loved her way back then. I also knew I didn't love my wife with anything near the intensity I felt for Jessie. My wife did me a favor cheating on me while I was away serving our country *and* when I was back stateside while my body healed from the rigors of war.

I was laid up for months recovering from the injuries I suffered at the insurgent's hands. The roadside IED had ripped through me and claimed the lives of seven of the best men I have ever known. I will *never* be the same. Sometimes I still wake up screaming, trying in vain to warn them.

It's crazy that my mind has pieced memories together for me that I couldn't possibly remember. Like the ringing stillness. There had been a moment of absolute silence when everything was still right before the blast. It felt like entire minutes of realization, but with the slow-motion inability to move or call out. Just the static-filled passage of time as it clicked by.

The reality is, there was no warning. No moment of stillness. No realization of what was about to happen. Griggs and McCarty had been arguing about whether or not getting a handy from another woman constituted cheating on your spouse. Then, in a flash, all I knew was searing pain and the rank smell of antiseptic. It felt like I was in a Full Nelson hold with a cement truck on my back. I can still smell the hospital sheets when I think about them. They smelled like hot, powdered ash, and my face was against them for weeks before I was stable enough to be transported back to the United States.

The USMC had shipped back an empty vessel, and Jessie gave me hope for the future. Hope that someday the agony of loss would let up its grip, if only a little.

When I caught my wife in our bed with another man, I was almost grateful. I couldn't stand to be around her anymore. The things the woman ranked as a level red threat were as trivial as fingerprints on the stainless steel fridge. I couldn't begin to unburden myself by sharing what a person sounds like when their lower leg has been blown off. Or how you can taste the metallic tang of your Lieutenant's blood as you shove gauze into the wound in his chest.

I couldn't do it anymore. I probably pushed her away with my emptiness and raw despair. But I couldn't understand why I had lived when my brothers had died. It's like I was spared so I could live to tell the tale. Except I couldn't tell it, it burned my mouth and tasted like ash. It also left an almost unbearable pressure on my back where skin grafts were healing, and muscles had been stitched back together. The ordeal overseas succeeded in vaporizing everything I used to care about. Everything except Jessie. She was my beacon in the storm, directing me safely back to shore.

She is the most beautiful woman I have ever seen. She is caring, she's fucking hilarious, and that *hair*. Her hair is a dark red that is so striking my dick swells just thinking about my fingers entwined in it. The amazing thing is, she has absolutely no idea how appealing she is to men. She never developed the pretentiousness normally doled out among the pretty people. Jessie isn't high maintenance like the women I tend to draw the attention of. She is down to earth, and just as self-deprecating as the rest of us.

The fact that I work very closely with her is a blessing and a curse, today it's a curse. She is wearing a tight black skirt that hits right above her knees and some heels with a strap around the ankles that accentuate her legs and remind me of a pin-up girl. I would say her top is inconsequential in its mossy greenness, but because I know what's beneath—with remarkable clarity, no top is truly inconsequential.

I have been struggling for a few months now, ever since the exposition party at 1462. That night marks one of the other times I have seen her naked. Not completely naked, well yes, completely naked, but she was painted like a warrior. Another image seared into my brain for all time. I swear she saw me from the stage, then looked me right in the eyes before she slinked down in front of me and spread her legs open.

The stage had been about waist height, so when she parted her legs and presented her pussy to me, I seriously considered burying my face in it and never coming up for air. The fact that she was covered with body paint did little to conceal her body from all the hungry eyes on her. For one thing, even if the paint *had* been clothes, they would have been very skimpy. If anything, the paint called attention to her tits and ass, never mind her delectable, open and begging pussy.

Pretty sure she had been teasing me, I was surprised to see the look of horror on her face and her instantaneous roll onto her hands and knees to crawl away from my thirsty stare. But then, she had slunk away from me sensually slow and all the while waving her bare crotch, even the unpainted parts, right at me.

My cock was responding to her display like it's practically conditioned to do. That is until that fucker, Silas popped up. She planted a kiss on him that I felt on my own lips, as well as in my slackening dick.

After the Goddess show, I was as confused as ever by her mixed signals. I swear she keeps me on the hook just in case Silas punks out. What she doesn't know, however, is that I'm no consolation prize. I have way too much pride and self-respect to play second fiddle to another man. Nope, once Silas is out of the picture, she is going to have to work for me.

It will happen soon enough, I know her too well. Once, she broke up with a great guy because he wore loafers. Another time, because the dude got up from his couch to fix the flipped up blinds—she was just certain he was too OCD for her. Seriously, it doesn't take much. An eye goober, the mispronunciation of "supposedly," a car that smells like cat pee…really, I could go on forever.

I already mentioned that I told her, I love her, but she doesn't have to know I would drink her dirty bath water. I just need to be patient. I'm going to let her get all the ridiculousness with Silas out of her system, and then she can challenge herself a little with me. That way, she can actually pine for something that stands a chance of working.

Silas is on borrowed time. He has already *literally* sexually assaulted her, leaving Jessie saddled with anxiety at best, PTSD at worst. Then there were those surveillance photos to further destroy the trust between them. I could actually buy a drink for whoever hatched that plan. Anyway, his time has to be just about up, the breakdown of trust in a relationship is the hardest to bounce back from.

Apparently, Silas gold medals in the sex department. Everyone talks about him like he is some sort of *sexual leviathan* or something, but I haven't seen anything all that impressive from him yet. I've watched him fuck her three times now, one she knew about, two she did not.

Now, before you start thinking I'm some kind of pervert lurking in the bushes, let me be clear, 1462 is an expansive bounty of sexuality. Sex and nudity drip from the ceiling like an interior sprinkler system. There are private rooms that cater to every fetish you can imagine, and even some you've never even heard of. However, the entire first floor is very, very public, and the club events are what legends are made of.

One such event was flashlight night, where the club was pitch-ass dark except for flashlights. A girl I hook up with at the club sometimes, Bradley, wanted me to attend the party with her. Now, Bradley had no idea I knew Jessie, but she was intrigued by the fact that the owner, *The Almighty, Silas*, was fucking in the public part of the club. She evidently had heard about his sexual prowess and wanted to observe what all the fuss was about.

5

When Bradley and I made our way over, Jessie was lying on an inclined liberator cushion with her hips at the top and her ass hanging over the peak of the liberator. Her knees were spread, and Silas was eating her out. Most of the flashlights were trained on her tits and her open thighs, but I wanted to see her face when she got off. So I waited, mesmerized by her writhing, naked body until she started to moan. When I shined the flashlight on her face as she came, I thought to myself, someday it will be me that makes her strain her head back and groan like that.

When Silas fucked her, it was pretty straightforward. No bells and whistles. Not to mention, the quick glimpse of his cock I saw proved he was no Dirk Diggler. I would say he is definitely bigger than average, but I've got more girth on him hands down. Her quaking tits were what I was most impressed with, so much so, that I missed her face when she came the second time. I imagine the blood had been pooling in her head the way her hips were raised, and I've wondered since if that had any bearing on the strength of her orgasm.

I never took her for the showy type, but to be fair, in that dark environment she was basically obscured. Not her body, mind you, but her person—Jessie Hayes was concealed pretty well. Not like the third time I saw her getting fucked, that was full Jessie, and I'll get to that, but first I'll explain the second time I watched her having sex with that douche bag.

She and Silas were in the mock interrogation room. There is a two-way mirror, but they really had no way of knowing if anyone was watching. It's not like the Peep Show rooms where as soon as someone locks the door to the booth, a red light turns on, so the performers know where to direct the show. I've fucked Bradley in there so many times I don't even care if people can see my scar anymore. It used to bother me a lot, but not anymore. I've performed in the Peep Show area when only one red light was on, and I've been in there when every single one of them was lit. Needless to say, Bradley *is* the showy type.

Anyway, back to the interrogation room. Jessie was handcuffed with her hands behind her back while she blew Silas. All I could see at first was his stupid ass, but when he moved, I saw her shirt was open, and her delicious tits were out and proud. There had been a few of us watching the scene from the other side of the mirror at first, but the rest got bored from the lame role play and left.

Eventually, with Silas sitting in the chair facing me and Jessie's cuffed wrists behind his neck, things picked up again because Jessie was taking control. She faced him, straddling his lap while Silas raised her skirt so that it only covered the top of her ass cheeks. She wasn't wearing panties, and I was straining so hard to see between her legs, I was probably fogging up the glass.

They were only about seven or eight feet away from me, and she had her ass popped out as Silas sucked on her nipples. The thing was, while Silas was caressing her ass, he would gently spread her for me— well, for anyone that happened to be watching but as luck would have it, it was just me. My dick was so hard having that view of her pussy that I almost left to find Bradley before they even had sex. Once she did finally lower herself down his shaft, it didn't take long. I was pretty disappointed in his stamina if you want to know the truth.

All of that nudity from Jessie, and witnessing all of that sex *still* doesn't even come close to the exposition party a few months ago. She was naked at that point in the evening because Silas had wiped most of the warrior paint off her tits and from between her legs. This time was different though because this time she *knew* I was watching. Besides knowing I was watching, she *one hundred percent* performed for me.

She looked me in the eyes the whole time Silas toyed with her body, and she held her legs open to me the entire time. When she sucked his finger, she licked and savored it like it was a dick, while staring right at me. When Silas turned her and deposited her onto the toy demonstration platform, she was disappointed to break eye contact and kept stealing glances back at me. She didn't even seem like she was enjoying it when he fucked her.

The exposition party was just another indication for me that Silas' time with her is limited. She wanted me that night, I could feel it.

7

Work the following week was intensely awkward because she shyly stayed in her office with the door closed. If she had questions or needed me for something work-related, she texted me instead of walking into my office like she normally would have. As time went on, the work atmosphere normalized again, and thanks to my keen ability to ignore the obvious, she seems back to the normal JB.

I feel like it's important for me to stay the course with Jessie. I know how she feels about me, and I know she is torn, but I will never accept the divided attention of a woman, I deserve better than that. I never want to have to convince her I am the better catch. If she never comes to that on her own, I can accept that. What I can't accept is dishonoring myself by trying to push her into choosing me. I could have easily had her the night I picked her up from the margarita bar, but I want no part of her breakup, and I'll not try to sway her.

Women are not a problem for me. I can get ass anytime I want it, but I won't settle down with the wrong woman again. I also never want to wonder if my girl is thinking about another man, and if Jessie doesn't end things with Silas all on her own, I would always wonder.

Chapter Two

Work

I knock on her office door as I'm opening it like always. She looks up at me with eyes the same color as her not-inconsequential shirt and smiles broadly.

"Hey, JB. I have your contracts. All the figures are spot on so don't waste your time checking my work," I match her smile and then sit down across from her. "Is this the month I get to start calling you, Baby Mama?"

She sighs, but keeps her smile, "No, it didn't work this month."

"It takes time, don't put so much pressure on yourself," I say, trying not to look at her boobs.

"I know, but I'm so full of Corey and Devin's sperm at this point, my body thinks I have a new boyfriend," she laughs at the last part, I don't find it quite as funny.

"Well, I for one am looking forward to your pregnancy cravings," then I tap my stomach, "I'm thinking of putting on a few pregnancy pounds too. You know, to show my support."

"That's kind of you, but you will really have to green light your eating habits. That, or stop working out," she says, and her eyes drift to my biceps then back up to my eyes.

"What do you think, potato chips for breakfast, a sandwich with tons of pickles on it for lunch—maybe ice cream for a snack?" I ask.

9

What she doesn't know is that isn't too far off from my regular diet. I try to eat clean dinners, but daytime eating already is a full green light for me.

"Mmmmmm, we should start our baby diets today," she says, widening her eyes and smiling a faraway smile.

"Easy, JB, it's only 8:30, there's still time."

She rolls her eyes at me. It's a habit she has when she wants to giggle like a schoolgirl, but puts the breaks on and looks away instead. I know that eye roll well.

"Is Silas supportive about you having a baby for Devin and Corey?" I ask. Maybe this is where she gives him enough rope to hang himself.

"Yes, he is very supportive," she says as she taps the contracts against her desk to straighten them. The action calls attention to her hands, and I see it. The ring on her finger. My mouth goes dry, and the compulsory ringing-silence closes in on me. Just like my faulty memory of the IED explosion, I feel like I'm caught in time and have no power to change the outcome of what's happening.

"I wanted to tell you about it after work," she says, knowing I feel like I've been raked over the coals and left to smolder. She knows there is no good way to tell me, and that the news will crush me and annihilate any hopes for our future. She does, however, have the courtesy to look dejected. She should, after so many mixed signals and unspoken encouragements.

It takes me a solid few minutes to find my voice, "*Congratulations*," I say, hardly above a whisper. I can feel the valves in my heart opening for a surge of blood and then closing behind it.

Her eyes fill with tears, and she reaches for my hand, "Salinger," her voice trails off, and she doesn't say anything else right away.

I pull my hand back before she can touch it, and then say, "JB, I just want you to be happy. I care about you enough for that." It feels like I'm hollow and someone else is controlling my voice like a fucking ventriloquist or something.

She starts crying for good now, "Salinger, I'm so—"

Oh my God! She is going to apologize to me. I can't take her pity, so I find the springs in my legs and stand up abruptly, "It's all good, Jessie. I'm gonna get back to work now," I say, and in what feels like one step, I'm out the door.

When I get back to my desk and sit down, I feel like I have absolutely no emotion to display. The word bleak is how I would describe myself except that might be too optimistic. But I can't let her know how broken I am. I'm not sure I can even admit it to myself.

For the rest of the day, I stare at one of my dual monitors and go through the motions of working. I skip lunch and only get up once to go to the bathroom, and when I leave, it's only when I'm sure Jessie has left for the day.

How the fuck am I going to see this woman every day while I'm dying inside? My entire being feels like it hardens, and that is only the beginning.

Chapter Three

Wrecked

By the time I get home, I have found an emotion, anger. How could I have put so much stock into her flirting with me when she was with someone else? I'm pissed at myself for being so confident she would tire of him. Did I miss some clues between all her affections and mixed signals? I'm such a fucking idiot! I played right into her hands. I *let* her keep me on the hook just in case Silas didn't work out. I put myself in this situation, and now there is nothing for me to do except fester and rot.

I grab Nash's leash from the hook by the garage, and he is at my side in a micro-instant. "Let's go, buddy, it's just going to be you and me for the foreseeable future," I grumble.

He picks up on my devastated energy like dogs do, and stops wagging his tail. He sits down politely; wondering if that will appease me. When it doesn't, he drops his head and follows me outside.

Nash is like a rock star in this neighborhood, everyone knows and loves him. Not a single day goes by that someone doesn't comment on his size or his unique coloring and good looks. He is still a puppy at nearly a year old, but his body is already a full grown Great Dane. He's a little knobby-kneed and gangly still, but I swear he fills out more every single day.

Besides his size, the other thing people always notice about him is his obedience. With such a big dog though, I had no choice but to make sure he was trained to behave right from the start. Now, he knows the drill. He will not approach someone without being invited, and he will sit and wait patiently for me to give him a command. If neither of those things happens, he will go wait in his bed until I call him over to me.

Mostly he abides by the rules. The one exception is when he greets me at the door to the garage when I get home because he knows I'm going to take him for a walk. I grant him this little indulgence because it's pleasant for me to have a warm welcome when I get home. It's nice to have someone happy to see me.

It's cold out, and I can smell snow in the air. The scar on my back always tightens up when the temperature drops. It makes me feel like if I fully extend my arms forward, the tissue of skin across the scar will tear right down the middle.

It's ugly, my scar. It takes up most of the right side of my back and continues around to the side of my ribcage. It's puckered and blotchy like scars are, and it took me years to let anyone see my back. It has a story like all scars do, that and every tattoo I have on my arms. Just like the names down the left side of my ribs, it's a part of me now.

They tell me I was lucky because bones and bodies heal, debridement procedures eventually end, and physical therapy doesn't last forever, but sometimes I wonder if I really was lucky. Beneath my scar, my ribs have been rebuilt with titanium metal plates and screws, my right kidney is gone along with part of my liver, and there is scar tissue on my lung from a pneumothorax and subsequent chest tube. That last little bit prevents me from doing all the cardio I used to or playing any contact sports with the guys.

Right now, Nash is doing his thing to attract attention and enamoring everyone within a two block radius. He has this gallant strut, and I swear he nods at everyone we walk past.

It's starting to get dark, but all the regular players are out, even a few that I suspect plan their runs around my walks with Nash. Sometimes, I even vary our route to see if Shelly and Erin materialize in their sports bras and tight athletic pants. They usually do. Tonight I'm out much later though, after waiting for Jessie to leave the office.

As if I conjured her up, I hear a runner's footsteps behind me. I guess Shelly based on her stride, but it's Erin.

"Hey, Salinger! You're out late tonight," she says as she passes me briefly before turning around and slow jogging backward. She keeps up the pretense so her boobs keep bouncing in front of me. It's a nice distraction from Jessie, but not enough of one.

"Yeah, I had to work late. How are you doing?" I ask with false cheer.

"I'm great! Hey, I have some beef stew in the crockpot if you want to swing by after your walk," she says, and it sounds rehearsed.

"That's so funny! I have dinner in the crockpot too," I lie. Avoiding the direct question is easier for me than making up an excuse as to why I don't want to swing by. Erin is a good looking woman, I just haven't had feelings for anyone besides Jessie for a long time. Not that I *need* to have feelings to fuck someone.

Just as I'm changing my mind, she responds, "Ok, well, have a nice dinner. Bye, Nash," she gives his head a cursory tap, then turns around and continues on her run. It's just as well, if I need sex to get my mind off Jessie I'll go to 1462, fucking a neighbor is a recipe for disaster.

I look at Nash, and he raises his un-cropped ears, readying himself for whatever is about to come out of my mouth.

"Let's head home, Nashy Boy." I pick up the pace and double-time it back to my empty house, Nash just lengthens his stride.

***

As I walk in the house, I can't help but wish I really did have something cooking in the crockpot. Wait, do I even have a crockpot? While questioning its existence, I turn on the gas fireplace to get some more heat going. The thermostat is already programmed, so it's not worth messing with it for one night.

As I tug open the fridge, more out of habit than hunger, I see beer, eggs, leftover chicken breasts, a wilted head of lettuce, and various condiments. I should be starving after skipping lunch, but I'm not. I grab the chicken and the bottle of Tabasco sauce. Nash takes interest from his perch on his bed and cocks his head.

"What? You know I have to eat first, it's an alpha thing. Blame the dog trainers of the world, I don't make the rules."

He shifts his head the other way as if the new vantage point will distort my words into something he wants to hear, like, *Are you hungry, Nash?* He lives for those words, those and *Let's go for a walk*, and *Squirrel*. Saying squirrel around him is downright comical. He drops his chest to the ground, leaving his tail wagging wildly in the air, and waiting for me to say, *Go get him*. At which point he scrambles for purchase on the hardwood floor like in a cartoon, then goes ripping out the back door to rid the world of all its vile squirrels.

I eat standing in the kitchen, no point in belaboring the task, and no point in dirtying any dishes. When I'm done, I feed the dog and let him out back, and then I go change into workout clothes.

My basement is my gym, I have all the machines and free weights I could ever need, and an ab tower that I call, *my bitch*. Tonight though, it's the punching bag that I'm interested in. I turn the music on loud to drown out my own pathetic thoughts and begin wrapping my hands and wrists.

***

I don't know how long I've been at it, but my hair is soaked, and sweat is dripping in my eyes. When I look up at the wall mirror, I look savage. The expression on my face is rage, my hair is hanging in my eyes, my tank top is stuck to my body, and my full sleeve arm tattoos stand out like billboards against my muscles. I'm exhausted, but not enough to not lie in bed feeling sorry for myself, so I tuck my chin and advance on the heavy bag again.

***

In the shower, I try to jerk off, but it's been so long since I've done it without thinking about Jessie that *no matter what* I picture, ends up circling back around to her anyway. I'm going to need to watch some porn just to be able to masturbate. I clearly need some new material. I'm also going to need to find something to fill up my after work hours because being alone with my thoughts will prevent me from ever getting over her.

That's what I need to focus on right now, getting over her. I have to shift my thinking from biding my time, waiting for her, to actively moving on. It's going to be incredibly hard seeing as I have to work with her every day. That ridiculous bobble on her hand will be a constant reminder and a new stab to my heart each day.

***

Once I finally get into bed, I'm hoping I'll fall right to sleep. That's the plan anyway, grueling workout, relaxing shower, the oblivion of sleep. As luck would have it though, oblivion is nowhere in sight. I try coaxing my penis to attention again, but I can't stop picturing Jessie's open legs when she presented her naked pussy to me from the stage. God, and her perfect swaying tits…I jump up, flinging the covers off of me and plod quickly into the living room with Nash, hot on my heels.

I need to stream the most unfamiliar porn I can find, it has to be the polar opposite of Jessie. Maybe a blonde? Or someone ethnic? Big girls? I even skim through the Hentai stuff, but that's too much like the Goddess body paint show. Jesus, I'm going to need to watch some 70's bush porn to steer clear of anything that reminds me of Jessie. What about anal? Yes, let's start there.

I start doing pushups in front of the fire, and pretty soon I have to remind myself that pornography is on the flat screen. I move to the couch, but I've already taken out my contacts, so I have to get up to go find my glasses.

While I'm standing in my underwear in front of the large window at the front of my house, I decide to watch my anal porn with the curtains closed, to preserve what's left of my dignity. There might be a slight stirring down below, so I'm hopeful.

I like anal sex, but I've never had it with someone I was truly invested in. I'm not sure I could do it with someone I love. Part of the draw is that primal need to claim, to possess…to own. But I don't want to own anyone, and I don't want to dominate anyone sexually, well, not in a D/s way. I need a partner who is strong in her own right. If she isn't, I'll walk all over her.

Like I said before, getting women is easy for me, but if there is no challenge, I start wondering if maybe I should have aimed a little higher. Maybe that's why I fell for Jessie so hard, that chick is nothing but a challenge dressed in tight jeans and a flirty smile.

I feel an unwelcome ache in my throat and try to clear it with a cough, but it's probably here to stay for a while, so I go grab a beer instead.

I settle in on the couch, this time I like what I see on TV, and my dick is definitely starting to surge to life. Stroking my cock is so familiar to me that I can get off in no time, but right now I really want to empty myself, both literally and metaphorically. I want to spurt all these raw emotions onto my stomach and then wipe them away. In fact, each time I come from now on I'm going to consciously envision myself moving further and further away from Jessie Hayes.

With anal sex on the screen, it's the visual of that moment of breaching entry that finally pulls my balls closer to my body. I can feel my cock distend, stretching the skin taut and filling my groin with warmth. Usually when I stroke myself, I just use a few fingers and focus my attention on bumping over the ridge of the head, but watching anal porn requires more of a grip because ass play is tight… and intense.

When I get close, I loosen my grip and slow way down. I really want to build myself up, so when I purge, it comes from the depths of my broken heart.

While I watch this guy slowly pump in and out of this women's asshole, I can remember what it feels like to be inside someone in that way, and my balls start to tingle a little, a very definite warning sign. I press my cold beer bottle against the shaft of my dick, and the tingling is mitigated, but the ass fucking is so raw and so insistent that I have to put my beer down on the coffee table. I cup my sack with the hand that's chilled from holding the beer bottle and grab my cock with the other hand, and then fucking crank it.

***

I try again to go to sleep, but the hurt and disappointment are too pervasive. I'm paralyzed with sadness and can't get out of my own head. So I decide to let Nash get on the bed with me. He is a poor substitute for a woman, but he'll have to do.

"Nash Potato! Come in here, Buddy," I call out to him.

He strolls into my bedroom looking confused but hopeful.

"Come on up," I tap the bed, "Come on, you can do it," I coax.

I can tell he is thinking about it, but he knows he is not allowed on the furniture, so his head is at war with his heart.

"It's ok, come on up," I tap again.

This time he hops up so that his front paws are on the bed. He is tentative, waiting for a correction that doesn't come.

"That's right, Nashy Boy, come on."

Now he jumps up all the way, and like a kid on Christmas morning, he can't control his excitement. His tail is going wild with the reckless abandon I've just afforded him.

The logistics of having a Great Dane in your bed are kind of like having a giant ferret…on crack, in your bed. First, he just spins around trying to find the best spot to get comfortable, and then he plops down like a sack of wet sand trying to sit on my lap, all 150 pounds of him.

"This might be a mistake," I voice out loud, as I try to slide the silver foothill on my comforter over to the other side of the bed. For a

19

minute he's all flailing paws and knobby knees, and in the chaos, he gives me a fat lip.

"I probably deserved that," I say as I bring my hand up to my mouth to check for blood. The sheets are light gray, and I don't want blood on the pillowcases.

Nash can't believe his good fortune, so he makes himself dead weight once he's lying down—just to stop me from dumping him off the bed. By the time I get him moved over and reclaim some covers for myself, I'm sweating from the effort. I lie back and roll toward him, so I'm spooning with my domestic pony.

He starts snoring, and I swear to God, he is pretending to be asleep, so I don't make him get down. "You're full of shit, you know that?" I say against his furry neck. I close my eyes and wonder how I could have been so wrong about where I stood with Jessie. Then the tears come.

Chapter Four

Work

I have to pull my shit together because I will never be able to face her if she feels sorry for me. Jessie tends to avoid uncomfortable situations, so it's up to me to right the ship. I need to march into her office just like always, ask an erroneous question and present myself as unaffected, maybe even upbeat. The first communication is critical—it's the most important because it will set the tone going forward. It will also be what she holds on to as she retreats into her denial of the situation.

Classic Jessie, first she ignores it and hopes the issue goes away on its own. Next, and perhaps the most damaging, she brushes it under the rug and pretends there is no issue. Which is exactly what I used to do. It took a great deal of therapy for me to face the loss of two entire fireteams. Denial is always easier because it's passive, and because facing something makes it true.

The chink in Jessie's armor, is that I know her so well I can play to her weaknesses. If I give her even the slightest excuse to ignore or deny the fact that she has wrecked me, she will seize it like a starving wolf.

With my head down, resting on my fists, I take a couple deep breaths. *You can do this*. I stand up, fill my lungs with air and hold it until my eyes start to bulge, then let it out slowly as I walk to the door of my office.

"Hey, JB. Do you have assessments for those properties up north yet?" My voice is strong, but I have to remind myself to unclench my jaw after I speak. I make a point to look her straight in the eyes even though my instinct is to look just above her head. She looks tired. Good, maybe she had trouble sleeping too.

"Not yet... Salinger—" she trails off and then looks away from my face. "I...I'm hurting too."

Fuck, she's going to derail me.

"Jessie, it's all good. Silas is a great guy. I'm happy for you, I was just a little shocked yesterday, that's all."

"Salinger, don't," she says, obviously knowing how I operate as well.

"JB, really, I'm ok. Can you just bring me those assessments when you're done with them?"

She deflates, "Sure."

***

On the way back to my office, I have to make a detour to the bathroom. I feel a little woozy and need to splash some water on my face. Thank Christ there is no one else in here. I pass the row of porcelain urinals and head straight for the stall. I don't even have time to shut the door behind me before I vomit in splashing heaves into the bowl.

After a few minutes, I stand up shakily and flush the devastation down the pipes. Then I rinse my mouth out and splash cold water on my face. I'm looking in the mirror, willing myself to get a grip when Jeff from accounting walks in the restroom.

"Hey, Salinger," he says brightly.

"Morning, Jeff," I volley back just as chipper, before pulling the door open and stepping back into the purgatory of my existence.

***

Back at my desk, I decide tonight is a good night to meet Bradley at the club. I pull up the 1462 website to see what's going on this evening, it's a slave auction. I've done one before, you basically give yourself over to be stroked and groped like an identity-less piece of meat.

I met a woman named Mary-Jane that night because we were both purchased by the same guy. By the way, it's not what you think, the club as a whole respects your limits and moderators are everywhere to make sure of it. My limits happen to include dudes, so even though Mary-Jane and I were auctioned off to a man, he took no part in the fun, he just told us what to do and we complied.

I've fucked Mary-Jane a handful of times since then. She's always a willing participant and a good distraction. Honestly, I hadn't planned on doing an auction again. I would consider it though, especially because I do feel like an empty shell, it might be nice to give over my body again.

I text Bradley: *Hey sexy, want to meet me at 1462 tonight?*

She responds right away: *Great, now all I can think about is riding your fat cock. I wish I could meet you, but I'm dancing tonight. Rain check?*

I keep it short and sweet: *Absolutely.*

By 'dancing,' she means stripping. Bradley is a full-blown exhibitionist, and to her, stripping is kitten play. She prefers to be watched while getting fucked. She is big into anal and is the one who introduced me to the whole gaping thing. Why someone would want their asshole stretched and left gaping open for an audience is beyond me, but I stopped trying to understand Bradley months ago.

She has sleeve tattoos too, very colorful ones. At first, I thought she was drawn to me because of mine, and she might have been initially, but what kept her attention was my scar. I suspect she had a painful past, though she never really opened up about it, and the huge scar on my back signified something to her. Maybe it represents something for me too. Maybe my totem should be a nasty, ragged scar. So far it's a pretty good representation of my life.

I'll try Mary-Jane. Same text: *Hey sexy, want to meet at 1462 tonight?*

Her response takes longer, in fact after working for a few hours, the vibration of the phone in my pocket startles me.

Mary-Jane: *Sorry Babe, I have my daughter tonight. What about next weekend?*

One thing I know for sure is that I will never go to 1462 on a weekend. That's when Jessie and Silas go. They play house during the week with his kid and then go tear it up on weekends at the club. Nope, I will not be going next weekend.

Yeah maybe, give me a call, is my response, though there isn't a snowball's chance in hell that I will go. I'll leave the ball in her court, then have plans next weekend if she actually does call.

Jessie pokes her head in, "Want to go to lunch?" she asks. This isn't unusual, we usually go at least three times a week. But things are different now, namely the lump in my throat and the empty cavity where my heart used to be.

"I'm still trying to get caught up, I might work through my lunch," I smile at her, even though my face would rather melt off my skull.

She looks disappointed, "Want me to bring anything back for you?"

"Not unless you go to Bruno's." I try to be dismissive—she is killing me with her sad eyes.

"I'll go anywhere you want," she says with conviction, but it's a damn lie because I counted on that and look where it left me.

"Ok then, a Philly cheesesteak." *Damn it, get out of my office.*

"Alright, I'll see you in a bit then," she says as she closes my door.

It's a good thing she's getting me a sandwich because it *almost* makes up for leading me on all this time, and then waving that fucking ring in my face. Actually, it is good she's bringing me food because I'll need something to throw up later.

Chapter Five

Auction

The auction isn't as crowded this time, but they do the same drill. They pass out cards with checkboxes on them for consent purposes. Initially, they divide the *slaves* up into groups. Last time there were three different groups. The mild batch, which meant no touching of any kind. The moderate one, which allowed touching but no penetration. And then, of course, my group—the adventurous ones.

Then they placed the card at our feet so more specific limits could be understood, like finger penetration but nothing else, or vaginal but no anal, no gags, no dudes, stuff like that. This time they may just use the cards, it's a small group, I'd say less than ten.

There are plenty of eager buyers though. The atmosphere is just like it is at any other bar, except they serve you your own alcohol. At first, everyone mingles, has a few drinks, sizes up the merchandise. Then the handlers take the slaves to another room to ready us for the stage.

Veronica is on the piano, she stands out like a choir girl among Cardinals, but not because of her dark skin tone, it's because she is an innocent little thing amongst all the debauchery. She is an employee of the club, *not an active participant*, as she has explained to me. It's a shame too because I'd like to have a taste of her chocolate.

I call her my *dark beauty*, and it makes her giggle and squeeze my bicep. I suspect she will someday do more than observe, but alas, today is not that day. She will, however, get an eyeful of me though, and that thought alone produces some warmth in the region of my dick.

As I sip on my beer and chat with the buyers, I'm happy to discover that there is not a single woman in here that I wouldn't fuck. There are, however, some I'd like to screw more than others. These are the ones I solicit with my witty personality.

I'm always a little nervous that I might not be attracted to whoever buys me, but because1462 is a very discerning club, that has not been a problem. Right now, things are normal, and we are among our peers. We don't become pieces of dangling meat to fondle until we get up on stage.

I've heard the club proceeds from things like the auctions and the webcam go toward stocking the bar with mixers. I personally think it would be nice to donate them to a worthy charity, last time I went for $600. I would be much happier knowing the proceeds of my degradation went to kids with Leukemia rather than equipping the bar with grapefruit juice and Pepsi. Although, I know one slave went for as little as $140, and he was an alright looking guy. It might have been his teeth though, braces as a kid wouldn't have killed him.

I wink at Veronica when she looks up at me, and she misses a few noticeable notes. I tease her with a little laugh that lets her know, I know she fumbled the song. It happens to be a very identifiable Pachelbel piece, and Veronica has never missed a note before. I'm glad she is not impervious to my charms.

Last time by this point I was crazy nervous, now, not so much. I'm kind of looking forward to some abuse, that way my outside can better reflect how I feel on the inside.

Cocktail hour goes on quite a bit longer than the allotted hour before the slave handlers tell us to finish our drinks and meet them in the bondage room in five minutes.

It's kind of extreme for me to use this as a distraction, but it will serve. I can't have another night like last night with only a few hours of sleep. Plus, coming to the club will remind me of all the other beautiful women in the world. If I happen to get my dick sucked, that's just one more opportunity for my body to rid itself of Jessie Hayes.

I finish my beer and excuse myself from the table of women, all of them solid eights at least. Back in the bondage room, the handlers have us get undressed and remind us of the rules. No talking while on stage unless asked a direct question, keep our heads down, and don't hesitate when asked to do something or the handlers will smack us with a whip or flogger. I might hesitate just for fun, in fact, *I know* I will hesitate just for fun. I didn't want to get hit last time, but this time I'm less invested in my body.

Some of the guys give their dicks a few tugs to get them going, not me. I'm fine going out flaccid, I will let the ladies elicit a response from me. A few of the female slaves are covering up and acting all coy, but it's just for show because two of them were here last time.

After going around to each of us and making sure they have the right cards, one of the female handlers says, "Ready, Y'all? It's showtime!" and proceeds to lead us out onto the platform. It's raised about two feet or so, placing our junk right about eye level with the buyers.

They spread us out for perusal first, then after about an hour of scrutiny, they will line us up at the back of the stage and then bring us forward one by one for auctioning off.

For now, I feel silly standing here stark naked under the bright lights. I'm more comfortable surprisingly, once the crowd comes forward and starts interacting with us. But right now, I can feel my penis swaying after being ordered to scoot over, and I feel like everyone is watching it, or waiting for me to give a speech or something.

The part I really hate is when they tell us to turn around because if my arms are at my sides, you can't see my scar from the front. Once I turn around, I can usually hear some of them recoil, and I can taste their pity.

Sometimes people will ask me about it, but for the most part, it makes them too uncomfortable to acknowledge it, so they don't. The tattoos are sometimes a surprise too. Usually, I'm wearing a button-down shirt, and because the tattoos stop at my wrists, you don't see them unless I want you to. Here though, there is no missing the scar or the tattoos.

I look toward Veronica and her piano but find that I am blinded by the spotlights and can see only dark figures. She is still playing, so I know she is here, I just don't know if she has seen me naked yet. That simple thought causes a tightening in my cock that I silently beg to stand down. I can't get hard yet, it's part of the fun.

The handler with the mic is a gorgeous brunette with big, juicy, red lips that I'd like to suck on. She is a regular at the club, and I believe I have seen her naked on the St. Andrew's cross, getting flogged.

"Good evening, Ladies and Gentleman, welcome to the 1462 slave auction." A round of cheers goes up. "I'd like to remind you of a couple formalities before we get started. First, you will respect the boundaries and limits of the slaves, or you will be escorted to the pavement outside by our lovely moderators, and your membership will be revoked. Secondly, this is not a scene or any type of role play. You will be bidding on the slaves with real money, money that you will part with before being given your slave. And finally, no matter how much you have paid for your slave, if they say *Red* or *Rumplestiltskin*, it requires an immediate reaction from you. Now, let's have some fun!" More cheers from all around.

"Why don't you all come forward and get more acquainted with the slaves, you'll need to determine the worthiness of our stock and the depths of your wallets."

As she walks past us to exit the stage, she lightly drags her fingernails across my back. At first, I think it's out of curiosity for what my scar feels like, but when I look back at her she smiles and mouths, *Yummy*!

Just then I feel a sharp sting on my ass and hear a command to keep my head down. I spin back around to face the crowd and am exceedingly-aware of what the sudden movement does to my cock as it sways to a stop. I think maybe I will *not* test the handlers today. That lash felt like burning hellfire across both cheeks.

Right away, a handful of women approach me. I'm blushing, but ironically it's not from having my naked dick level with their collarbones, it's because I'm embarrassed that I got smacked. It was a cane, and those skinny ones hurt like a motherfucker. I'm not even sure if my back could take a caning. The scar tissue is hard, but it feels to me like the flesh is paper thin, not to mention the agony I was in for so long. Just the thought of pain radiating from that spot makes me break out in a cold sweat.

A warm hand cups my balls and jostles them a bit. The threat of injury to my testicles immediately redirects my attention from wondering if I should try to tell the handlers not to cane my back, to the intense, dull ache that is looming just around the corner. One squeeze would buckle me to the floor.

"Very nice," a sexy blonde says. She has an accent that sounds German, or maybe Austrian.

Blood is thinking about filling my penis but doesn't actually start the march to my prick until another chick slaps it. I'm not surprised by the slap, that's the thing about being up here, at any moment pleasure or pain can be inflicted. I find myself cautiously waiting for either, but always with my guard up. She slaps my cock again, I think just to watch it flop around and dangle there.

"Turn around, sexy man," the first woman says, and it sounds like she is purring.

Shit, here goes. I turn around slowly and wait for the shock to subside, only there doesn't seem to be any. Maybe these ladies have already seen my scar. Perhaps from a peep show booth.

"Tell me, slave boy, have you ever had a woman's tongue in your ass?" she purrs.

Now, I *am* shocked. "Uhh. Nooo," I answer nervously.

She drags her tongue across what must be the long red welt from the cane, dipping her tongue lightly into my ass crack in the process. "Why don't you bend over for us? Hmm? Show us your tight asshole."

Now I am very uncomfortable. Last time, someone stuck a lubed finger in my ass and massaged my prostate, but she didn't make me bend

29

over in front of her and *present* my butthole. I'm frozen in place for a second before the fear of the cane overwhelms me, and I bend over a little.

"Don't be shy, anyone can stroke your dick. I want something even more personal from you."

My heart is racing, I don't think she is kidding.

"Now, bend over more. Carefullll, the handlers are watching."

I bend over more, purely out of fear of the cane across my scar. This is singlehandedly the most humiliating thing I have ever done, and I've streaked naked across the high school football field with a couple of teammates before a game, while the band roused the crowd. We even did a little dance in front of the cheerleaders for Christ's sake.

There's a gaggle of women standing behind me right now waiting to see my asshole. Fuck. I consider saying RED, but I would never be able to show my face in here again.

"Now spread your legs," she says slowly.

I do it, then feel a hand press between my barely parted thighs and again handle my nuts. Against every attempt to stop it from happening, I can feel the blood start to surge into my constricting cock.

"More, Darling, I need to reach your extraordinary penis."

I do as I'm told, but only because a handler is on the move. I can't believe what this has come to. I will certainly be beefing up my hard limits after this ridiculous shitshow. I can see the boots of a cane-wielding guy to the right of my vision, and I can tell he is watching me. With my ass to the ladies, any caning would hit straight across my back.

I open my legs more, and I'm positive the stance is now displaying my shy asshole. The heat in my cheeks matches the heat in my package as I continue to engorge. *Fucking traitorous cock.* She jostles my sack and then reaches her hand much farther forward, where she drags her fingernail up and down the bottom side of my stiff shaft.

Then, with a force stronger than natural gravity, she bends my dick down, forcing it back between my legs. Right above the base of my penis, at the bottom of my abdomen, there is a forceful but dull pain, kind of like a pulled muscle. The position is definitely not natural for a raging hard-on.

"Back up, so I can taste you," she whispers, and I close my eyes, fearing what an asshole might taste like.

Instead, she closes her warm, wet mouth around the head of my cock, and slides her tongue back and forth across my frenulum. Maybe this isn't so bad. My dick is becoming an uncomfortable steel rod, and my sack is being pressed against my body in a borderline painful way that still feels good.

"Ummmm, you taste warm and inviting. I'm going to put a glans ring around your penis in a minute," she says before she closes her mouth around the tip again. My dick is stretched so far back while being fully erect, that if she lets go, it would snap back and hit my stomach. On one hand, it hurts, but the attention to my f-spot is driving me crazy.

She slowly directs my penis back to its rightful position, facing north, well, it would be if I wasn't bent over with my hands on my knees. Right away, I feel her spread my ass cheeks and lick my hole. I gasp at the invasion of what should be private. I have never been rimmed before, and honestly, I've never wanted to try it.

The sensation, beyond mortification, is wickedly soothing and highly erotic. Feeling her warm breath and wet tongue glide around, I'm trying not to like it, for decency sake, but it feels wet and good.

She only rims me for a few alarming seconds before she pulls back, slaps my ass and tells me to turn around. When I do, I'm disgusted to see quite a crowd has gathered.

"That's enough, Marta! If you want him, then buy him, but give the rest of us a chance to test him out," this comes from a feisty brunette, one of the ones I was hoping to shag tonight.

"Yes, I agree," comes a voice I recognize, just as Veronica steps forward and pushes to the front. Oh hell, I hope she didn't witness my rim job. Seeing all these faces rejuvenates my humiliation, especially in front of her. She plays the piano, she doesn't participate in all this crazy shit!

Before the embarrassment runs completely through me, she reaches out and takes hold of my bobbing erection. The shock I felt being rimmed for an audience is eclipsed entirely when Veronica slaps my cock against her tongue five or six times and then closes her luscious mouth around it.

My head falls back as I slide in and out of pure bliss. I groan, but when I feel my balls start to tighten, I snap out of it. I can't get off this soon, so I have to employ every trick in my arsenal to chase the climbing arousal away.

Jessie is going to marry Silas. There it is. Nevermind the hummer I'm getting from the beautiful pianist. I'll never get one from Jessie.

Orgasm averted.

The feisty brunette steps up, and when Veronica gets a little possessive, feisty advances too and then sucks my left nut into her mouth. Shit, this is intense. My thoughts feel muddy, and it's hard to concentrate.

"We are almost out of time, let's get the ring on him," the rimmer says. Then two intoxicating mouths release me. With their retreat, I'm wet, and as the air hits that wetness, it helps cools down the building heat in my groin.

I don't know what a glans ring is, but I can guess. My glans is the head of my penis, so I imagine the ring goes around my coronal ridge. It sounds amazing. Then I wonder if Veronica is going to bid on me? All of a sudden the thought occurs to me, and I'm excited by the idea of her being an eager participant.

Rimmer squeezes between the women and shows me the ring. It's not a full ring but about seventy-five percent of one, with a silver ball on each end. She attempts to slide it over my helmet, to a wave of laughter from the ladies. Then she stretches the two balls further apart and then forces it around my shaft like a cuff. It sits right at the base of my glans with each ball pressing against the sides of my frenulum.

The pressure of the balls on that intensely sensitive spot brings a shit-eating grin to my face. With my dipstick at full salute and a glimmering ring around it, I'm sure the buyer will be very satisfied with the merchandise. I'll work these little titanium balls right up against her g-spot. This night just took another unexpected turn, I wanted to be distracted, well…I'm distracted.

"Ladies and Gentleman, please take your seats. Hopefully, you've all gotten a good look at 1462's wares and are ready to begin bidding," the beautiful Master of Ceremonies announces. "In case this is your first auction, I will quickly run through the process," she says, as she looks over at me, obviously down to my erection, then back to my eyes with a smile. "I will be bringing each slave forward one at a time. Should you see one you'd like to bid on, you simply raise your paddle; there is no need to shout out like barbarians. If you happen to be the highest bidder, you make your way over to the dashing man standing right over there," A man in a dark suit waves his hand and gives a nod. I think he is one of the guys that runs admissions. If you ask me, he looks like a tool. He always wears his hair back in a ponytail, and I've seen him wearing his aviator sunglasses inside the club.

"Once you have been divested of your funds, you will be given your merchandise to do with as you please—while obeying their limits, to… the… letter. We are a civilized lot, you see?"

They move us to the back of the platform, and I take my first good look around at the other *merchandise*. The two women who were all submissive and shy backstage continue the charade with their heads down and nervously shifting their weight. I hate mousy women. Why some guys prefer a meek, submissive woman, I will never understand.

Between the sub-y girls are another woman and a dude. The woman stands proud as a peacock, slowly rotating at the waist to fully showcase her b-cup and pierced nipples. I've been with a woman with pierced nipples before, and her nips were so sensitive I could hardly touch them, she didn't even like my chest pressed against her while we had sex. Sweet girl, I think she is still a kickboxing instructor.

Anyway, the guy is toned but really skinny, so his gigantic, monster dick looks extra out of place. It's always those skinny guys that surprise you. Maybe his member wouldn't look so huge on a bigger guy, but on him, it's disproportionate to say the least. He will probably go for a hefty price. Little good it will do him if he doesn't know how to wield it though.

On the other side of me are two more girls and two more dudes. If I get purchased with someone again, I hope it's the one with long black hair. I've never been with an Asian woman before, but her—her I would fuck every day of the week and twice on Sunday. The other girl is pretty too, she's your standard blonde with blue eyes, tiny waist though, with a belly chain around it.

The guys are both better than average, one has—

"Alright, let's get started shall we?" the MC asks in a loud voice that breaks into my thoughts. She walks over and takes the hand of the chick with the belly chain, then walks her forward, front and center.

"I'm going to start the bidding at $50, do I hear $50?" A handful of paddles go up.

Ok, back to the last two guys. One has the look of an IT professional that likes to get spanked in his off hours. He is fit but otherwise average. The last guy is striking. He is obviously of Native American descent, and I think I saw him in the body paint fashion show. He has bands tattooed around his biceps and on his forearms that, along with his long black hair, add to the Indian mystique. He looks pretty fierce until he smiles, then his expression tends toward boyish. He is the best looking guy up here and will probably go for the most money.

My dick is throbbing, and the ring is just a bit too tight. Last time they left me up here until the end, I'm really hoping I'm not last this time, I think my cock head would turn purple before then.

The MC turns the blonde to the side, so she is facing her and lifts her tits with both palms, appraising their weight or something.

"These breasts are so firm, you should feel them they are exquisite. Do I hear $250?" I'm glad to hear the bidding is getting up there, I've not been paying attention. God, my dick feels heavy, I can't stand here all night with a boner and this ring, the word engorged doesn't even do it justice, it feels more like an overfilled water balloon right before it pops.

"Sold! For $325," the MC says as she leads the blonde across the platform and holds her hand while she walks down the step. Then she turns and walks straight over to me. Thank God.

Before walking me forward, she flicks the balls on the base of the ring, twice, in quick succession. The force of the flicks knocks my cock backward toward my abdomen, and the balls shoot two zingers through the bottom of my dick head. I'm not completely sure if the whole thing hurts, or if it feels good, kind of both.

She threads her fingers through mine and walks me forward. "I just might bid myself," she says under her breath before she raises the microphone to her lips.

"I'm going to start the bidding at $200, do I hear $200?" A flurry of paddles shoots up. She cups my balls and lightly rolls them around in her palm.

"How about $300?" She is jumping right in I guess. There are fewer paddles this time, but still a respectable amount.

"$400?" Only two paddles left now. "Whoever ends up with him is in for a treat, just imagine these balls stroking your pussy from the inside," she says with wanton desire while looking me in the eyes and dragging her finger around my coronal ridge, right where the ring butts up against it. I bet this woman is a lot of fun in bed.

"$450?" an extra paddle goes up, now we are back to three.

"$500?" she asks without looking away from my eyes. I'm supposed to be looking down, but I can't seem to.

"$550?" one paddle remains steadfast, another hesitantly goes up. Neither are Veronica and surprisingly, neither are the rimmer. I guess she had her fun for free.

"$575?" last paddle up, it's the feisty brunette that sucked my left nut. Now, I'm really excited, she was one of the ones I was hoping for.

***

When we get to the private room, there is nothing in it but an oriental rug and a sectional couch. Huh, I expected more from a private room in this club. The others I have seen have been very fetish oriented and often waaaay over the top.

She closes the door behind us but not all the way, and she certainly doesn't lock it. Another surprise for me, but I suppose privacy is not her thing. At this point my erection has mostly gone down, I'm still a little stiff, but the engorged water balloon feeling has pretty much dissipated. However, the glans ring is still a noticeable presence I'm not yet accustomed to.

"What's your name?" I ask, and it's the first time either of us speaks.

"Rebecca. You?" she asks.

"Salinger." I'm not sure where to go from here and have never been one for awkward silence, so I lean in and kiss her. Briefly at first, then more. I love that there is no pretense here. No, *should I kiss her or be a gentleman?* No, *Is it too soon to want to fuck her?*

I got married really young, right out of college in fact, and we had been together since the middle of our freshman year. Consequently, I'd only had sex with two women before getting locked down, so if it seems like I'm a bit of a man whore, you'll need to adjust your compass. Before the club, I had never had sex with someone I didn't care about first.

1462 is a bit of a slippery slope though. For the most part, I try to keep it to the same couple girls. Oral sex is different though, I'm not as discerning about head. If you've ever had your dick sucked, you know what I mean.

Not having to pussyfoot around the matter at hand is refreshing, so I start unbuttoning her shirt right away. While I have one hand at the back of her head, my other fingers go to work on unhooking her bra. She shoves it down her arms, and both of my hands go immediately to her tits.

While skimming her nipples with my thumbs, my building erection starts to make itself known. As the veins in my penis are constricting, preventing blood from leaving my cock, I'm feeling almost primal, and lust is clouding any judgment I may have entered this room with. I move my mouth to her rigid nipple and flick it with my tongue a few times before sucking it hard.

"Oh, Yes, I want to feel your teeth," she groans.

I tug on her nipple with my teeth as I pinch the other one, harder than I normally would have, but she seems to like things a little rough. With my free hand, I try to shove her skirt down, but there is a zipper, so I need to engage both hands.

I get on my knees to slide her skirt down while I drag my tongue around her bellybutton and kiss her stomach, now and then lightly sucking and biting her skin. She smells like lemon body wash, and it makes me want to taste her all over.

My cock is throbbing now, and all I can think about is getting her caught up as quickly as possible. After enduring the hour-long, crushing boner on stage and now being faced with her soft skin and hard nipples, I feel like I'm going to lose it.

Her fingers are roughly in my hair, and she squeezes her hands into fists when I slide her panties down. The tug on my hair follicles gives me a little shiver as I dip my tongue into her crease. I lift her thigh over my shoulder in order to open her up for my tongue and then I melt into her pussy.

"Guess who's here?" comes a voice from behind me. Confused and pissed off by the interruption, I pull my face from between Rebecca's thighs.

"Oooo, ahhh, don't stop," Rebecca pants before she continues, "I have a surprise for you."

"Ok," I say with caution, as I watch the Native American guy march in with the complete diametrical opposite of himself. What I mean by that, is that she has short, wild blonde hair and skin the color of snow. She's cute, but I don't remember seeing her downstairs.

"That's right, we get two for the price of one," the new girl says, which makes the dude laugh. I know I said he was good looking when we were on the platform, but I have no intention of having any cock myself.

"I need to feel your tongue again, Salinger," Rebecca moans. I hesitate while I observe what the other two are doing. The woman strips out of her clothes while he takes a seat on the couch, watching her like he wants to light her up. She walks over and straddles him while his face goes directly between her tits. *Two for the price of one*? Looks like I might be able to check group sex off my list tonight.

I get back to the task at hand by sliding the tip of my tongue through Rebecca's lips, then finding and sucking on her clit. This isn't the best position to eat someone out because I can't really get in there, you know, to the silky part.

"Suck it harder," she says with conviction. I've got to say, I've never really sucked that hard on a woman's clit before. Usually, I find them to be too sensitive, but, I aim to please, so I comply by sucking it harder.

She comes within about a minute, and then I graze my teeth over her swollen clit as I back up. There is nothing like a women orgasming right against your mouth. Having such tremendous control over someone in this most basic way is very powerful.

"Now, I need you to fuck me," she says as she takes my hand and leads me to the couch. My knees ache like an old man's after kneeling on the hard floor, but now it's looking like I'll get to sit down. That is, sit my naked ass on a cold leather couch which God only knows who else has sat their naked ass on.

I think fast.

"I want you from behind, so these little titanium balls will graze against your g-spot."

She looks intrigued but still doesn't move. She may be used to calling the shots.

"Come over here." I press the issue by taking her wrist and guiding her to the arm of the couch. Then I direct her to slide her legs apart with a nudge from my foot and press her forward over the thickly padded side of the couch.

Seeing her bent over like this, with her legs wide open is such a turn on. She is so vulnerable right now, so trusting. Her unguarded pussy is glistening wet and just begging for me to plunge my cock in. It would feel so good to squeeze in there, all tight and wet, or even just to play with her silky vagina lips with the head of my dick for a bit. I won't though, not without a condom.

The club has huge glass containers of rubbers everywhere, and there is an expectation of the guys to wear them. Not that I have to be told. Besides the possibility of STD's, what I fear most is getting a woman pregnant. Let me rephrase that, I'd love to get a woman I'm in love with pregnant, someone who I want to be with forever, and watch our kids grow up. But I've gotten a woman pregnant before, and it's something I will never recover from.

It was the summer before going away to college. My first real girlfriend. We dated most of our senior year and thought we were in love. Neither of us had ever had sex before, so we didn't care about STD's, and pregnancy seemed like such a distant threat back then. Anyway, we wound up having a lot of sex, both with and without protection and found out she was pregnant pretty soon after graduation. We were both terrified, I was set to go to Duke on a football scholarship, and she was going to go with me. She had planned on attending a community college until she could get residency, then was going to transfer to North Carolina State University.

I would have left my scholarship, found a job and married her if it would have made her keep our baby. I couldn't accept that she wanted to have an abortion. That was *my baby*. I begged her not to go through with it. I even offered to raise the baby by myself. I would have done absolutely anything to get to see my kid grow up.

I started having panic attacks knowing I couldn't change her mind, and that I would never get to see or hold my child. The day she did it, I refused to go with her, or drive her, or have anything to do with it, I couldn't even get out of bed.

I ended up going to Duke in the fall without her, and at the end of January when the baby would have been born, I got my first tattoo. I know in my heart he was a little boy, I can't explain how I know, I just

39

do. I named him Aiden and carry his memory forever on my left arm, by my heart.

"Fuck me, Salinger," the command snaps me from thoughts of the past, and I go to retrieve a rubber from the jar on the sideboard.

When I get back, Rebecca is still bent over the couch, she has her arms behind her back as though she were cuffed, so after I roll the condom gently over the ring and down my shaft, I grab her wrists tightly with my left hand.

I ease in slowly, pressing all the way into her tight, welcoming embrace. The ring increases the friction against the very sensitive portion of my dick and feels fucking amazing. She is soaking wet and very willing, so I just start pounding into her.

There is no love here so I can fuck her for the pure carnality of it. I'm done giving my heart to women who just hand it right back to me with a big, fuck you. Maybe I'm not cut out for love. I'll just take all my emotions, all my hurt, all my fucking baggage, and concentrate it into one thing. Sex.

I'm fucking her hard, it's an angry fuck, but she loves it. She's all kinds of vocal too, and even waved away the other chick when she wanted to trade. I'm getting close, so I have to slow down. Rebecca likes it rough, so I grab her hair and give a slow yank until she gets my meaning and stands back up.

"I love how you fuck me!" she cries out, "I don't want you to stop!"

I ease out anyway, it's time to check the next box. I go grab another rubber because I'm not sure how the next chick feels about sharing all of Rebecca's juices.

She gets off the other guy and takes the condom from me. Against my better judgment, I sit down naked on the leather and start to ease off the rubber. The second it's off, her mouth is around me. I can't help but watch her as she glides up and down my dick. I'm still not used to the glans ring, and when extra attention is placed on the little silver balls, it's almost enough to make me howl.

Rebecca saunters over and hops on the other guy's dick with no concern for the previous juices, and then brings her head to his shoulder.

My new girl slurps off my dick and says, "You taste yummy." Then she rolls the new condom down, stands up, and climbs aboard. She lowers herself down faster than I would have liked and it makes me suck in my breath. It's not that it hurts; it's just that the feeling of first entering a woman is so magnificent as you bore through silky resistance, that I like to languish in it a bit. But this approach works too.

She arches her back and places her hands behind her on my knees while she gyrates against me and waves her tits in front of me. Automatically my hands go to her boobs. They are on the smaller side, so I drag my palms roughly up and down against them, feeling her hard nipples scrape against my palms.

We are looking into each other's eyes, and the whole thing seems pretty intimate, so I ask, "What's your name?" It feels ridiculous to ask such a thing because my cock is already deep inside her, but I've never fucked a woman and not known her name.

"It's, Ashley. And you're, Salinger," she says as she grinds her hips more, squeezing her vagina around me and pressing the balls tighter against my frenulum.

"Yeah, we didn't bother with any formalities did we?" the other guy laughs, "I'm Carter, and you are?"

"Rebecca, now fuck me like Salinger did."

The grinding is becoming too much for me, and Ashley hasn't come yet, so I help her to turn around, so she is leaning back against my chest. It's time to get after her g-spot.

She starts moaning almost immediately, so I begin plucking at her nipples. I'm pinching them pretty hard and tugging them forward until they pull out of my grasp, then I do it again, and again until she is whimpering, "Yes, awwwwwww, just like that, yes!" She's getting close, but so am I, dangerously close.

I can't come before her, I can't think about her wet pussy slobbering all over me. *Oh, shit!* My balls tighten, and I start to feel the waves coming. Just as I start, she cries out, and I can feel her vagina pulse all around my dick, from every direction, milking semen from deep within my body. The glans ring is borderline too much, as I feel my body shiver with its last spurt of cum.

My penis is almost grateful to go soft after being on high alert for so long. Ashley adjusts herself in my lap, so she is sitting sideways like a child. We are both hot and sweaty, so the transition is a smooth one. She lays her cheek against my chest while I absentmindedly toy with her nipple.

Then Rebecca speaks up, "Salinger, I hope you can rally because I want to feel that glans ring in my ass while Carter fucks me."

Carter laughs and then says, "You dirty little whore! Can't get off without DP can you?" he says this teasingly as he tisks his tongue, not disrespectfully at all.

I look over at Carter, "What are the mechanics of that?"

"I'll lie down, she'll ride me cowgirl while leaning forward, and you'll fuck her in the ass," Carter says.

I reflect on that for a moment, I thought only porn stars wanted two huge dicks in their body at the same time. Anyway, what I had meant by *mechanics* was, won't our dicks be rubbing together on either side of a very thin wall? And won't our ball sacks be slapping together? I decide not to voice these questions out loud, but they are still at the forefront of my thoughts.

"I'll get you ready," Ashley says as she coaxes the spent rubber off my cock.

I tip my head back against the couch. This isn't me. I don't do this stuff. My eyes spring open when Ashley nearly swallows my flaccid dick. Right away I start to feel the clenching that indicates blood is on the march to my sleepy member. I guess this is the new me, no emotions, just a dick to get fucked by.

***

Carter is lying down on the couch, and Rebecca is fucking him cowgirl style while Ashley gives me head. The tip of my penis is exceedingly sensitive, so even after just blowing my wad, I'm ready to go in pretty quick succession. And by ready to go, I mean my cock is primed and ready, not necessarily that I'm ready for my first threesome…with another dude. In my fantasies, it's always been two women, never like this.

Carter is spreading her cheeks and telling me to, "Come fill up this tight asshole with your thick cock." Rebecca is leaning forward on his chest and arching her back in a very pornographic way. The way her back entrance is presented, it's like a neon sign blinking at me, and Carter's direction is like a runway attendant guiding an airplane safely to the gate.

Ashley rolls a new condom on me, pours lube into her hands, and then greases up my cock. When she looks up at me, I half expect her to smack me on the ass and say, "Go get em, Champ," like some sort of offensive line coach or something.

I make my way over to them while Rebecca croons, "Fill up my asshole, Salinger. Fill it up good."

Ashley is ready with the assist and pours lube straight onto Rebecca's hole. Then she starts fingering her butt while I eyeball Carter's nut sack, lying not too far below my entry point. I'm somewhat amused by the fact that this is precisely the porn I watched last night, and now I'm right in the thick of it. I guess visualization really can open some doors.

Alright, cue the distraction. This is the new me, the walking penis—seeking release in any form. Here goes. I drag my cock head around Rebecca's anus to pick up a little more lube, then I place my tip right at the threshold. My position is a little screwy, because I have to have one knee on the couch right between Carter's hip and Rebecca's shin, and the other foot planted on the floor with my knee a little bent and my quads tight. I'll probably end up with an interesting cramp to tell the tale.

I press in a fraction of an inch then pull out. When I press again, I go very slow and stop each tiny bit to let her sphincter relax.

"That feels so good!" Rebecca laments, obviously not in any serious pain. I keep up with the slow pace, and once I get the helmet of my dick fully passed her initial resistance, I need to stop longer to collect myself. Her ass is so tight it's squeezing my tip from every direction, and with the extra pressure from the glans ring, I'm probably not going to last long.

Carter's thrusting has stopped, but he continues to spread her cheeks, leaving his hands righteously close to my junk. This is probably for the best because seeing the proximity of his fingers helps temper the excitement of my dick.

I ease in slowly a little more, I can feel Carter's dick on the other side of the wall, and I know he can feel mine with the glans ring, but to be honest, the tightness of her ass feels so good that I'm not too concerned with the additional penis. I still don't want our sacks to touch though, and as I get closer to being all the way in, the possibility grows.

"Fuck yeah, you are filling me so good!" Rebecca almost chants. When I fill her all the way, I have to stop again. This is a ton of sensation, and the ridge of Carter's cock is pressing on the ring even more.

I begin sliding in and out very gently because the resistance against my dick is so delicious I'm almost dizzy. This is where things get a little weird though, because Carter begins groaning from my movement along with Rebecca's mewing. I'm positive the balls of the glans ring are stimulating Carter, and it makes me feel like I'm fucking him too.

Ashley does her part by straddling his face, which quiets him down a bit and also causes him to move his hands to her ass. Now I'm spreading Rebecca myself and am not as hesitant to be all the way in.

Carter is mostly leaving our rhythm up to me, which is for the best because both of us thrusting would get a little sloppy. What he is doing instead, which is a little bit of a mind fuck, is grinding against my penis as I ease in and out.

With four of us in the mix, there is a lot of noise. The girls are very vocal, Carter is muffled, but vocal, and I'm even moaning as I try to keep myself from coming.

"Oh, Fuck yeah! Those metal balls on your cock are insane!" Carter groan-shouts, and it marks the first time a dude has ever talked to me during sex, let alone while referencing what my cock is doing to him.

I hear a muffled, "Oh, yeah. Ahhhhhh, fuck, yes!" and then Carter comes. I can feel his dick pulsing as it pumps out his load. Before his penis even softens, Ashley follows suit while throwing her head back and screaming to the ceiling. I'm verrrry close too, but I'd like Rebecca to get off first, so I risk touching Carter to reach around and mess with her clit.

We both come simultaneously. The contractions of her vagina radiate through the thin wall and are added ripples to my own surges of semen spurting into the tip of the latex. The slipperiness of my own cum added to the tightness of her rectum makes me want to stay in there all night.

We all lie here in a heap of hair and appendages, too wiped out to even move. I can't even pull my penis out, I just let it soften and get pushed out from her tightness. I don't even care that I'm all tangled up with Carter, and I'm pretty sure my ball sack is touching part of his anatomy.

As our panting slows, Ashley and I are the first to get up. I guess that makes sense because we are the ones on top. Rebecca rolls off next and slides to the floor with a huge smile on her face. Damn, she has great tits. Carter stays where he is, too spent to move.

"That was the most intense sexual experience I have ever had," Carter says flatly. I secretly wonder if this is the direction I should take in life. No worries at all, just continue to feed my primal nature with meaningless, though amazing sexual encounters. Maybe I would have more interpersonal success if I just follow my dick around like a divining rod searching for water.

***

When I get home from the club, it's after eleven, and I need to get up at five thirty if I'm going to work out. I set my alarm for six thirty, I got enough of a workout in tonight. Nash is sitting by the edge of the bed waiting for an invitation and hoping last night wasn't a fluke.

"Ok, Nashbrowns, you can come up." I don't even fully have the words out of my mouth before he jumps up and snowballs himself into a clump of legs and fur in the middle of my bed.

"You are going to have to learn not to be such a bed hog if you plan on sleeping in here every night," I say as I bulldoze him over to the side. He acts like a sack of wet concrete and doesn't help me a bit.

As I start to doze off, I chuckle to myself.

Rim job…check.

Group sex…check.

Threesome…check.

Double penetration…check.

Daisy chain…check.

Christ, I'm a whore.

Chapter Six

Distance

The last few weeks have been a struggle at work, followed by an intense workout, then porn, or the club. I have succeeded in detaching myself almost entirely from the act of sex. I'm really just feeding a need, or scratching an itch now. It has become very mechanical for me.

I have been burned by nearly every woman I have ever cared about. I've also been burned caring about friends too, the names mark their presence in my life as ink down my ribs. Anyway, if you haven't put it together yet, that's why I tend to keep people at a distance.

The truth is, as my therapist has pointed out ad nauseam, I am so terrified to lose someone I care about again, that I subconsciously keep everyone at arm's length. His theory may have a scrap of truth to it, but maybe I'm just more of an introvert. I mean, I have friends, I play in a flag football league in the summertime, and I do fantasy football every season with my college buddies. It's not like I'm a total loner, I go to too many bachelor parties and weddings to actually believe I don't have any friends.

My family is pretty small. My dad passed away thirteen years ago, my little sister lives in San Francisco as an advertising executive, and my mom moved to Florida last year. So the fact that I'm not surrounded by family doesn't exactly point to me keeping people at arm's length.

I used to take my mom to Sunday brunch at least once a month before she moved, and I dropped everything to go to San Francisco when my sister's longtime boyfriend broke up with her. So it's not like I'm full of unhealthy relationships, or lack emotional bonds with people, I'm just an introvert, that's all.

However, perhaps my tendency to keep people away is being encouraged a little more lately. I have been spending a lot of time at the club fostering empty relationships, and I love it. I've turned over a new leaf, and it suits me really well. I even stuck my dick through a glory hole and got sucked off by a stranger a few days ago, the only thing I know for sure is that it was a woman, because, you know, limits and all. I can literally not think of a more detached sexual act than that. It's great, and the distraction is helping me get through the work days that I have to spend with Jessie pretending I'm fine with the fact she is going to marry Silas. So the club helps me fill my time and numb my feelings, it's a win-win really.

Once I can leave the office, I'll run home to eat and take Nash out, then it's off to the club for obscurity night. I've never been to one of these parties before, but I guess the first floor of the club is pitch black and people interact and explore each other in total concealment. Sounds detached, and perfect. I may or may not get my dick wet, we'll have to see how I feel once I get there. I just need to wrap up a few things here at work, pop into Jessie's office to deliver my obligatory witty statement that demonstrates I am doing just fine with her engagement, and then disappear into the obscurity of the club.

***

So, it's dark alright. I can't see my hand in front of my face. From what I can gather I'd say there are probably about thirty people in here. I've been told conversation is encouraged, but apparently, names are forbidden.

Now that I'm here, I'm a little worried my brain will just turn some miscellaneous woman into Jessie. That would set me back a mile if

I allow myself to fantasize about that, it would be easy to do though, shit, you could have an erotic tryst with anyone your mind could dream up.

I guess the idea is that if you remove some sensory stimuli, your other senses will be heightened. So far that appears true enough, that or someone just bathed in hairspray because that's all I can smell and it makes my throat feel tight. I don't like overly done-up women with tons of hair and makeup, I like a more natural beauty. I guess one exception to that is that I like when a woman has her fingernails done. I'm going to sound like a pig expressing this, but it's so hot seeing manicured fingers wrapped around my dick while she's giving me head.

"Excuse me, I'm sorry," a woman says after bumping into me.

"That's all right, I think that's what I'm here for," I respond.

She laughs then says, "You sound handsome, can I touch your arms?"

"I guess. I think my leprosy has mostly cleared up," I answer. She giggles, but what are you supposed to say in that situation? That must be why women hate when a guy asks if he can kiss her. Just fucking do it already.

She reaches out and finds my shoulders, then slides her hands to my biceps.

"You're taller than I thought," she says. I don't know what to say to that, so I don't say anything. She is sizing up my arms, and it occurs to me, she is assessing whether or not I'm worthy of her company and if I comply with her high standards.

"Do I pass your test?" I ask, and it sounds really cocky even though I don't mean it to. I guess I'm becoming more and more jaded as the days tick by.

"I don't know yet, all I can feel is your shirt."

"Then why don't you do something about that?" again really cocky. She should be so lucky.

She finds the buttons on my shirt and starts undoing them one at a time. When my shirt is hanging open, she slides her soft hands all over my chest and then pushes the shirt off my shoulders. I help by pulling my arms out of the sleeves and letting the shirt drop to the floor.

She walks around me, touching me all over my chest and back. If she has ever seen me here before, she now knows who I am, because she lingers on my scar. She caresses it with her hands, kisses it softly multiple times and then drags her tongue around it. She kisses down my back and lingers for a bit just where my lower back sways. Her kisses are very delicate, and for some reason, that spot is very ticklish, so I feel like squirming, but I hold still anyway. There is a rush of heat to my genitals which is the alarm sounding for the incoming surge of blood.

She makes her way back around to my chest. So, now she knows who I am, I wonder if I can figure out who she is? It's time for me to do some reconnaissance of my own. I put my hand on the back of her head and pull her into a kiss. She doesn't sound like someone I know, and her hair doesn't feel familiar, it's long and smells fruity, but I don't recognize anything about her. Our kiss is sensual and completely engrossing, it's exciting to kiss someone so passionately but not be able to see them or even know if you have ever met before.

My hands find her breasts. She is wearing some kind of tight, V-neck shirt with the base of the v almost all the way down to her bellybutton. Her cleavage is ample, and I'm not too sure she could wear this top to the grocery store because so much of her boobs would be visible. She has the size of tits that guys like to picture their dick in between, and, yep, no bra. I pull back from the kiss and lightly scratch my fingernails over her nipples, making them swell from the contact. As she starts to respond more, I increase the pressure of my scratching nails until I can't stand that her nipples are still behind the cotton of her shirt.

I spin her around and hold her ass against my hard-on while I open the v of her shirt and expose her tits. My hands are all over them, I love the feel of a hard nipple grazing against my palms.

When she starts to grind her ass into my erection, I drop one hand and slide it down the front of her skirt, into her panties. She is already soaking wet, so when I slide my finger into her tight pussy, there is a slippery resistance that I want to feel with my cock. I didn't think ahead enough to actually have a condom on me, so unless she has one, her clenching vagina will only feel my fingers tonight.

She tries to turn around, no doubt for my cock, but I prevent her from doing so. Then I start rubbing her clit. Between her eager pussy and her amazing tits, I'm ready to bend her over and fuck her till the lights come on. She squeezes her legs against my hand then silently comes, almost violently onto my fingers.

When she turns around, I wipe her pussy juices all over her nipples, then blow on the wetness before sucking one into my mouth. Her hands are in my hair, and I'm slapping her nipple with my tongue when it happens. I picture myself with Jessie.

The crushing disappointment that washes over me softens my dick and almost has me spitting out this woman's nipple. The fact that it's completely dark makes it really hard for me to snap out of the visualization. I've seen Jessie's breasts, and they are similar in size to these, so all I can think is that this is exactly what Jessie's tits would feel like in my mouth. This woman smells good and has soft skin, just like Jessie, she is moaning and making sounds that I wanted Jessie to make with me.

"I think it's time I returned the favor," she says into my mouth as she kisses me and palms my dick through my pants.

"Actually, I've got to go, but thank you for a fun night." It sounds horrible, even to me. As I turn to leave, I feel like I took advantage of this woman and then was like, *later*! But I really have to get out of here. I think she's too stunned to speak at first, but I hear her protests behind me as I make my way out of the room and down the hallway to the alley door.

Chapter Seven

Party

When I got the invitation to Jessie and Silas' engagement party, I had to go downstairs for a couple of hours. When I came back up all sweaty and pissed off, Nash was even afraid to come near me. I can't decide what's worse, being invited to the God forsaken thing, or *not* being invited.

Either way, here I am, at the rented-out martini bar, to celebrate the wondrous occasion, and rub elbows with all their family and friends.

I've dutifully made the rounds and made charming small talk with Jessie's parents and brother and sister. I met and discussed football with Silas' father and brother, and I've told each of Jessie's friends that I've met before, how great it is to see them again. I congratulated the happy couple, hugged Jessie, and shook Silas' hand. I deserve a fucking Academy Award.

"How is your martini?" someone asks, and it snaps me out of my sulky ruminations. I turn around to see Corey and Devin. I smile the first genuine smile of the evening and give them both the guy hug with the slap on the back.

"I've had better," I say, and they both know I'm not talking about the martini.

"Let's sit down," Corey suggests, as he nods to a tall cocktail table.

"I'll get us another round of drinks, you two stay put," Devin says, then hurries off.

"You know, my mom always used to say, God answers prayers in one of three ways. Yes. Not yet. And, I have something better in mind," Corey says, his eyes are kind and seem like they see right through all the bullshit straight into my soul.

"Your mom sounds like a great lady," is all I can say because I'm a little choked up.

Devin comes back in a swirl of energy and sets three fresh martinis on the table, then he inclines his head forward conspiratorially, "You know, the divorce rate is like sixty percent these days," he says with a curt nod. He is smiling like a hyena, and I know he is kidding, and trying to bring some levity to the situation, but we all laugh, and it makes me feel a tiny bit better anyway.

***

I step out back to get some air. It's chilly out now that Autumn is so far underway, so all the table umbrellas were taken in weeks ago. The patio tables themselves remain, as do the lit up strings of white lights above the flagstone patio. I step to the railing and watch the bustle of the city. I wonder how long it will take for me to be able to see Jessie without feeling the twist of the knife?

I've switched from martinis to a bottle of pale ale. Beer is really more my style anyway, and I've done enough pretending for the night.

"Hi stranger," comes a woman's voice. I turn and see Jessie's girlfriend walking toward me.

"Hey, Paige. You need some air too?" I ask.

"No, actually I just came out here to keep you company."

"Is that right?" I have nothing better to say. Paige is beautiful, but any sort of hook up with a friend of Jessie's would feel too incestuous right now.

"Yeah, I thought you could use a friend right now," she says. Jesus, does everyone know the dynamic between Jessie and me? She has a really flirty smile on her face as she closes in on me.

"Paige, I—" I start, but she leans in and kisses me. I don't kiss her back at first, but then I get worried about hurting her feelings, so I give it about twenty percent.

"Salinger, you are so...incredibly...sexy. I just can't help myself," she says as she unzips my pants and, I swear to God, takes out my dick right here.

"Paige, no."

"Stop, Paige, I can't—"

"We can't do th—"

Those are my protests. They demonstrate the exact space of time it takes for me to succumb to her warm mouth. My cock is conditioned now to perform like a trained monkey, so it's certainly up for the challenge.

Paige is actually really good at giving head, which is just as well because I can't have this taking too long. Shit, the scandal. *At Jessie's engagement party? Right out in the open?*

I come right into her mouth, and she surprises me by swallowing it down. Then she stands, tucks me back in, zips me up, and says against my ear, "Jessie has my number," and then walks back inside with the feel of my warm cum in the back of her throat. I'm utterly stunned by the whirlwind that was my exchange with Paige when I hear a slow clap.

"That. Was. Awesome."

A woman is approaching me, and if I get the gist of it, I think she is teasing me.

"Can we pretend you didn't see that?" I ask, feeling shy and wishing I could go back and delete this whole fucking night.

"Nope, it's burned into my brain now," she smiles. I've never met her before, I would remember.

"Well, there is no hope for that. It will just have to stay there," I laugh, but surprisingly it's not out of embarrassment. Now that she is closer to me and hot, it's kind of sexy knowing me getting a blowjob is burned into her brain.

"I guess it will have to stay. How do you know these two knuckleheads anyway?" she asks as she leans her forearms against the railing too.

"I work with Jessie."

"Oh, YOU'RE Salinger," she says with unnecessary emphasis. Damn it! Am I carrying a billboard or something?

"What does that mean?" I ask, but I'm pretty sure I don't want to know the answer to my own question.

"I just heard that Jessie has a smokin' hot co-worker named Salinger. Now, aren't you glad you asked?" she says, seeing my relief and maybe a little bit of modesty.

"Oh," is all I can say even though it's lame.

"I thought the almighty Salinger wore sexy glasses?" she says in the form of a question.

"I usually only wear them at work because I look at a computer screen all day. I do own contacts you know."

"Shame, I might have recognized you sooner," she smiles. Her eyes are very green, which seems unusual for someone with brown hair. They are also lit up by the string lights overhead and definitely laughing at me.

"How do you know the happy couple?" I ask, genuinely interested for the first time tonight.

"I grew up with Jessie and Devin, but I only moved out here a few months ago, so I haven't known Silas for very long."

There is a long moment of silence while we each ponder what to say next.

"Are you thinking about giving me a blowie?" I ask, and we both crack up laughing.

"What's your name?" I ask once the laughing fit subsides.

"Avery."

"It's nice to meet you, Avery," I say as I shake her hand.

Chapter Eight

Invite

I've been feeling pretty good the last few days, so when Jessie pops into my office and sits heavily in the chair across from me, my stomach doesn't fall into my shoes.

"What's up, JB?" I ask.

"I've been doing a lot of thinking."

"Oh hell," I glance back at my spreadsheet and type in the last few entries, then look back at her.

"Salinger, I think you should come for Thanksgiving," she delivers this notion like an atom bomb then sits back in her chair to watch the fallout.

"Come where?"

"To my place."

"Why would I do that?" I ask, and the question is sincere.

"Because you mean a lot to me and this is the first year I won't be with my family for Thanksgiving."

"Sounds cozy," I snort. How cute, Silas, Ruby, Jessie, and the pitiful Thanksgiving orphan, Salinger.

"It won't be," she leans in and puts her elbows on my desk. "Cozy, I mean. It will be Silas, Ruby, Devin, Corey, Corey's mom, possibly Analise, a few of Devin and Corey's friends, and Silas' brother, his nephews, and sister in law..." she ticks off names on her fingers, then looks at me expectantly.

Instead of answering her, I ask, "Why isn't your family coming this year?"

"They were all just here for the engagement party, it's fine. Will you come?"

"I'll think about it," I say noncommittally.

"Great!" she says as she stands up, "Oh, and Salinger?"

"Yeah?"

"Bring a pie."

***

When I get home with some bags of groceries, Nash looks at me expectantly. Apparently, he has grown accustomed to me bringing him marrow bones from the deli counter.

"Listen, buddy, marrow bones are a privilege, *not a right*," I scold. He raises his ears and cocks his head. "Just kidding, here you go," I hand him the bone and he happily trots out back to gnaw on it while I figure out how to bake a pie.

Jessie's invitation to Thanksgiving is going to get in the way of me sitting on the couch all day Thursday watching football, but I guess I have to get used to the idea that she's off the market, but still my friend.

The club has helped me sever my wayward notions about a happily ever after, and I'm finally able to be around her without wanting to throw up on my shoes. So, I've decided to consider Thanksgiving a type of immersion therapy.

I figure, I'll bake a pie tonight, and if I ruin it in any one of a thousand ways, I still have tomorrow to try again. Plus, if I need to, I can always invite one of the runners home with me after my walk with Nash. Anyone who owns a crockpot probably knows how to make a pie. Maybe I should wash my sheets, just in case.

Chapter Nine

Thanksgiving

Ruby and two little boys open the door when I get to Jessie's. As promised, Ruby is very precocious. She sticks out her hand and introduces herself and the boys; Sawyer and James before she allows me to enter. Then the three of them scurry off to wait by the intercom to buzz in the next guest. Looks like they take their job as gatekeepers very seriously. As soon as I step inside, Devin swoops in and hands me a beer.

"I'll take those," he says, referring to the pumpkin pies with homemade whipped cream, that came out perfectly the first time, thank you very much.

Corey is by my side in an instant. These two are great at anticipating that I might be a little uncomfortable.

"Salinger, I'd like to introduce you to some friends, and also to my mother," Corey says as he absorbs me into the group. "This is my mother, Maribel. Mom I'd like you to meet my friend, Salinger," he says.

"Oh, Salinger, I've heard so much about you!" Jesus, does my name precede me everywhere I go?

"Maribel, it's a pleasure to finally meet you. Corey has shared some of your words of wisdom with me, so I feel like I already know you a little bit," I smile brightly, and she giggles shyly. Moms always love me, it's a gift I have.

"And these are some friends of ours, David and Paul, and Brice and Stephanie." We all shake hands, and I immediately feel welcome.

"Salinger! You're here!" Jessie calls out before she charges over and throws her arms around me, then kisses my cheek.

"Wow, JB, did you hit the liquor early today?" I ask before I shake Silas' hand. I wonder if he recognizes me from those damaging photos? He doesn't seem to, but he could just be feeling a little cocky because he put a ring on it.

"Not really, come! I want you to meet my girlfriend, Avery, she just moved here from Seattle." Ahhhhh, Avery is here. The evening is looking up already. Jessie grabs my hand and actually drags me away to find Avery.

Avery is talking to one of the little boys, so she is squatting down when Jessie and I hit her airspace like a hurricane.

"Avery, this is Salinger!" Jessie says this as if connecting two dots from a long line. Kind of like, *This* is the one I have talked incessantly about.

Avery stands up and smiles at me, "So I see."

I smile too. The facial expression feels foreign to me, so I hope it doesn't come off goofy or artificial.

"Oh, you two know each other?" Jessie looks puzzled, and I'm suddenly *really* nervous about what Avery will say.

I'm still grinning like a baboon, so Avery says, "Well, sort of. Salinger was in the middle of losing an argument. Actually, he didn't put up much of a fight. You know, now that I think of it, his protests were pretty weak."

"Avery," I say, just to stop her from talking for a second, "It's really hard to argue with someone who simply doesn't listen to other people's objections, or read any of their cues." I'm still smiling.

"That's very true, especially when the cues are so mixed. Right?" She is teasing me, this feels familiar from her.

"Salinger, what were you even arguing about?" Jessie asks, waaaay too invested in this conversation.

"Politics."

"Sports."

We both respond at the exact same damn time, so Jessie squints her eyes at me. Feeling like I need to pull the pin on this grenade, I look at the kid Avery had been talking too. "Are you Sawyer or James?"

"Sawyer."

"How old are you, like fifteen?...Sixteen?"

"Noooooo, I'm four and a half!"

"Sawyer, why don't you show these guys your huge bin of Legos? I need to go make some gravy," Jessie says, dropping it for now, but I guarantee she will revisit this particular discomfort on Monday.

"You have Legos?!" I say with excitement. Sawyer grabs my hand and starts to pull me away from Avery, so I grab her by the hand and say, "Oh no, we're in this together."

"Sawyer, Avery here appears to excel at dishing things out, should we see how well she can take it—with a boys against girls build off?"

He smiles and looks dubious. Perfect.

"Ok, you go grab your brother and Ruby, and I'll map out our attack." The kid actually gives me a thumbs up, then runs off to go get the other two.

"You're pretty confident in your skills, aren't you?" she asks, and I detect a little sexual innuendo. Or maybe not, that could just be the club's influence on me.

"Well, have *you* ever built a Star-Wars-Imperial-Super-Star-Destroyer? ...Hhmm?" I ask with wide eyes.

"No. But what I lack in skill, I make up for in *style*."

"Duly noted."

***

With the addition of Avery, my evening is looking up, and I'm having fun. No, seriously. I'm having fun. However, when it's time to sit down for dinner, both Sawyer and James turn out to be total cock-blockers. Their mom has the flu and had to stay back at the hotel, and their dad sat down right between Silas and Corey's mom. Consequently, both boys want to sit by me, the little turd-burglars. Devin and Corey sit across from me, probably to buffer me from having to sit across from Silas and Jessie. Rounding out our end of the table is Avery, who sits on the other side of little James.

Throughout dinner, Devin, in a way that only Devin can, proceeds to pepper Avery with questions on my behalf. I say on my behalf, because of the way he looks at me every time she says something noteworthy about herself. Almost like a grandfather would nudge you in the ribs and nod at your grandmother's back, just to remind you to tell her how wonderful her canned string beans are.

"A flight nurse, is that right?" *Nudge, nod, did you hear that Salinger?*

"That is a very noble profession, heroic, in fact," *Nudge, nod,*

"Did you know Salinger is a highly decorated Marine? Very noble and heroic indeed." *Nod, wink.*

"Careful Devin, Salinger and I are liable to stand at attention and burst into the Marine's hymn," Corey says, in an effort to derail Devin's blatant obnoxiousness.

"Both Marines? Did you guys serve together?" Avery asks us both but looks only at me.

"Our deployments overlapped a little, but we were in different Battalions, and at different bases. Corey's unit was an artillery unit, mine was infantry."

"Wow, thank you both for your service," Avery says. "What were your jobs while you were deployed?"

"I was an explosive ordnance disposal technician," Corey answers as he quickly glances over at me. He may be the only one to notice the sweat on my brow and recognize the faraway look in my eyes.

"I was a rifleman," I say flatly.

"So, Avery, tell us more about being a flight nurse...Is the job what tempted you away from Seattle?" Corey dives in, valiantly steering the conversation away from our deployments. I appreciate him for doing this more than you know.

"Well, it's either really boring or really exciting. There is no in between. And no, it wasn't the job that brought me from Seattle. I just, well, I needed a change," she says, and I can tell there is a story behind why she moved and based on her discomfort regarding it, I can tell it's a big one.

This is the point in the evening when Jessie throws her chair back and runs to the bathroom to blow Thanksgiving chow.

"I think Jessie may be coming down with the flu too. That's exactly how it came on for Jill, fine one minute, and barfing her brains out the next," Sam says.

"Humph, pity. That just means more pie for us," Devin says, to a round of laughter.

With the Devin-led interrogation over, I'm drawn into conversations with some of the other guests, which is automatically more comfortable because Silas is gone, checking on Jessie.

***

The twins are exhausted, their incessant chatter from the beginning of dinner has all but stopped, and Sawyer is ready to fall asleep in his delicious homemade pumpkin pie that is a huge hit, by the way.

I'm talking to Stephanie about dog training because apparently, she has a little dictator at home that thinks he's the boss. I'm explaining that she doesn't need to be aggressive with him, but rather she should utilize a few alpha tactics, like making sure she always enters or exits a door first—before her dog, always eats first, and doesn't let him lead the way when she walks him. I started alpha training Nash from the start because he is naturally an alpha dog. We've had some comical scuffles when he used to try to lead the way out the door, namely with me pinning him to the door jamb with my leg so I could go first. Sometimes I even broke a sweat in the tussle, because he was a determined little shit, but he never went first. Now he is the best-behaved dog at the dog park, which is important because he is also the biggest.

"That makes so much sense. Do you think it's too late to alpha train hi—"

This is when little James glances down, and then pukes right in his lap, I even get some of the splatter. His dad jumps up and hauls him off to the bathroom while the rest of us listen to his vomit slide off the chair and dribble onto the floor. It's not the look of puke that's so offensive, although Thanksgiving vomit is a real treat with all the different colors and textures, it's the smell, so I'm trying really hard not to stand up and strip off all of my splatter-wear before running out the door.

Jessie and Silas still have not returned, and now we are down two more, one of which is the parent. So I think the hierarchy for vomit clean up naturally falls to Devin as one of the other inhabitants of the condo, but based on his look of vapid disgust, I'm guessing maybe Corey?

Simultaneously, we all place our napkins on the table and slide our chairs out. For the most part, everyone begins clearing the table while discussing how nice it is that we were all finished eating. Not me though, I'm afraid of my full stomach with the proximity of warm, fragrant puke. Avery is a nurse and probably conditioned to deal with vomit and much worse, so I'm aware I can't honor my authentic self and run from the stench while pinching my nose.

When Corey approaches the offending pile of vomit with a roll of paper towels, no one is more surprised than me when I go over to help. He's been such an unspoken support for me with the whole Jessie thing, as well as detouring the conversation when it threatened to hit a vital artery for me. He's just too kind and good to leave him alone to the task. I do my best to hold my breath while cleaning up the same chunks I helped James cut at dinner. The plan is a good one until I have to suck in air to breathe again, which leaves the smell bottled up in my nose.

"You don't need to do this you know," Corey says.

"And leave a fellow Devil Dog to do it himself?" I ask.

After we have cleaned it up and wiped the floor with bleach wipes, I take off my button-down shirt, leaving my tattoos visible under my navy t-shirt. There are usually mixed reactions when people see them for the first time because I'm so clean cut, no one ever expects them. I knew

Jessie for *years* before she ever saw them. Long-sleeved shirts were just better for me at work, and I never want to have to explain myself. Each one of these tattoos means something to me, and I will never make excuses for them.

"I didn't realize you were such a badass," Avery says as she approaches us with a sly smile on her face.

"Are you referring to my vomit-cleaning skills?" I ask, playing dumb even though I'm positive she is referencing my tattoos.

"UmHm, that," she says sarcastically, while feverishly nodding her head. I think she likes that I'm full of surprises.

"Well, I think we are going to get on out of here. The food is all put away, and the dishes are done except the last load for the dishwasher," David says as he and Paul put their jackets on. Corey hugs them both, thanks them for coming and apologizes for the unexpected turn. I think everyone is so afraid of catching the flu, now that the seal has been broken by David and Paul, it will be a mass exodus.

Avery and I work on returning every last Lego to the bottomless Lego bin as Sam rounds up his sleepy boys, and wrestles them into their jackets.

"I'm really sorry to have brought the plague to Thanksgiving dinner," Sam says as he shakes all of our hands. "Let Silas know I'll call him in the morning."

"Sounds good, Sam," Corey says as he hoists Ruby up into his arms. She is half asleep, so she is floppy like a ragdoll before she tucks her face against his neck and snuggles into him. She is almost seven years old, much bigger than the twins, but Corey is such a formidable guy, she still looks like a small, delicate child perched on his hip.

"Honey, I'm going to run your mom home, I'll be back soon," Devin says to Corey as he helps Maribel into her coat.

And just like that, we are down to just the four of us.

"How about we open another bottle of wine?" Corey suggests over his shoulder. It's not really a question because he is already halfway to the kitchen to get it. Avery and I sit on the sectional, and she slides out of her shoes so she can tuck her feet under her.

"This is more my style of Thanksgiving right here," Avery says, and I have to agree. Everyone was incredibly nice, but you never really want to be *that* guy at someone else's holiday gathering.

"So, do you agree that the boys and I totally kicked your ass at Lego building?" I ask with a completely straight face. "I mean, it's sorta obvious don't you think?"

"I wouldn't say it's *obvious*, but your jet fighter may have had a few bells and whistles that our storefront did not," she smiles. She is really beautiful, but I'm having a hard time shifting gears from the sexual gluttony of the club.

I seriously feel like I need a detox period before anything that smacks of a respectable relationship can begin. I'm not even sure if I'm ready for this whole get-to-know-you thing that's happening right now. If she were a member at 1462, I'd already have bent her over a spanking bench and had her six ways from Sunday. I do, however, acknowledge these are not the thoughts of a sexually healthy human being, so, there's that.

Corey comes back with upside down wine glasses between his fingers and a bottle of wine. The fact that he is still holding Ruby as he goes about these tasks makes me smile knowing that Jessie is going to have a baby for him. He will unquestionably be a fantastic father.

"So, did you guys decide to scrape the lot and start over, or are you going to gut the house and start from there?" I ask. I know they have big plans for their newly purchased house because from what I hear it's a diamond in the rough, with an emphasis on the rough part.

He lays Ruby down next to him on the couch and covers her with a blanket while I open and pour the wine.

"The plan for now, is to gut it, but depending on what we encounter along the way, it still might end up a scrape," he answers.

"I've seen Devin's CAD designs, it's going to be fabulous," Avery says, and it reminds me that she's been friends with him for a long time, Jessie too.

"I hope we can have it finished before a baby comes though. Can you imagine the three of us living here with an infant?"

"Don't you think Jessie will move in with Silas? Especially once she gets pregnant?" I ask and for the first time, thinking of Jessie moving with Silas, I don't feel the twist of the knife between my ribs.

"Yeah, I would think she would move in with him too," Avery adds.

Corey looks thoughtful, and then says, "You know, I think there is a part of Jessie that feels like she would be cheating us out of the experience if she moved out."

"Maybe," I say, and then think of how special Jessie is for doing this for them. She would even live here, stacked up on top of each other, so as to not *cheat* them out of the pregnancy experience. At least my picker wasn't off, she really is as amazing as I thought.

"I bet you're right, that sounds like something she would do," Avery says. Then she casually puts her hand on my forearm and asks, "What about you Salinger, do you want babies someday?"

Alarm bells sounding. This is not the time or place for *that* conversation. I scramble for an appropriate response, "Uh, yeah sure."

Thank God Devin chooses this moment to walk in, he has a way of entering a room like a full marching band, and it saves me from having to elaborate or admit that, yeah, I want kids someday, almost more than I want my next breath.

"I could get used to this. Everyone else cleaned up, now I can sit back and enjoy some wine with friends," Devin says, as he sinks back into Corey's side and raises his feet to the coffee table. Then he goes on, "What do you guys think, a double date? I think a double date."

Holy shit, he's as subtle as a Las Vegas hotel implosion.

"Devin, you're so pushy. When did you become such an orchestrator? Oh wait, never mind, since birth," Avery says, only now removing her hand from my arm. I feel like an uncomfortable teenager sitting on the couch between his prom date's parents, waiting for his date to finally come down the stairs.

"I think that would be fun," Corey says. Traitor.

"Yeah. Devin, where should we go?" I ask, trying really hard not to gut punch him. He is making this feel awkward when there is no need for it to be. If I want to fucking ask Avery out, I can do it myself. I *am* a grown man, last I checked anyway.

"Paintball," Avery says, and suddenly I'm back on board.

"You know Salinger is a rifleman, right? And Corey is no slouch with a gun either," Devin says as if to warn her.

"Don't worry, Devin, your delicate skin will only bruise for a few days, and I've heard you get used to the sharp sting of the paintballs," Avery says with a huge, teasing smile. Good, it's not just me.

"Ok then, paintball. Next weekend," Corey says.

"Yea! A double date!" Devin sings. He is so loud, Ruby even stirs a bit.

"I'm going to check on Jessie and Silas. Devin...why don't you get Ruby to bed in our room, we can sleep on the couches tonight," Corey says. He widens his eyes ever so slightly at Devin to drive home his meaning, but I think I'm the only one who notices.

After they leave the room to their respective tasks, I say, "I'm getting the impression you are a little bit competitive."

"I have three older brothers, it comes with the territory."

"Do I have to worry about them kicking my ass?" I ask as I shift on the couch to face her better.

"Not if you are good to me," she answers.

Then I lean in and kiss her. See?...a grown man.

Chapter Ten

Demands

Work has been busy the last couple of days because I've been pulling Jessie's weight too. Turns out they all got the flu, courtesy of Silas' sister-in-law, Jill. It's hard to keep us both caught up while maintaining my steady pace at the club though.

I'm pretty committed to 1462 this week. I've been nailed down by both Bradley and Mary-Jane to meet at the club tonight and tomorrow, respectively. I guarantee Bradley will want to do some exhibitionist type fucking, either on the peep show stage or right out front and center in the main room. Mary-Jane likes the private rooms more, but if I'm honest, I'm not really into all that role play shit. We've done the whole doctor/patient thing, I've spanked her as my naughty student, and taken advantage of her as a cop while she tried to get out of a ticket, the list goes on. Really though, it's a case of the ends justifying the means, because I'm there for the sex, not the improv session.

On top of all that, my group sex crew wants to have a repeat performance, and all three of them have been hounding me to pick a day that works with my schedule.

I still won't go to 1462 on a Friday night or at all over the weekend, so that means the next three nights are going to be club nights, and then on Saturday, I'll go have a respectable date with Avery.

I've felt very conflicted about the whole date thing, well, not the date really, more like my whoring around. Don't get me wrong, I *am* interested in pursuing a relationship with Avery, it's just that I feel so, so…what? Impure maybe? I know that sounds ridiculous, but the fact that I have put so much energy into making sex about fucking and lust, instead of about exploring possibilities, or having any feelings of being connected to a woman, that I feel like I have to now detach from the club lifestyle, just to be fit for a potential relationship.

I really feel like I need a detox phase, I wasn't kidding when I said it before. I am not looking for the 1462 lifestyle to be the way of my future. I utterly and completely want to fall in love with someone, have a family, and grow old together. I don't need all the pomp and circumstance of being sexually adventurous. I mean, I'd like to be sexually adventurous with my girlfriend or wife, but I don't need bondage rooms or sex parties.

In fact, I don't even like the man I've become. I have detached from the considerate guy with empathy and compassion for others, and I've become someone I don't even recognize anymore. I have never been the guy who leads with his dick, I've always been the guy who leads with his heart, usually to my detriment.

I guess I felt like I needed to pack up my heart for a while so it wouldn't feel like such a piñata anymore. However, in shielding my heart I have now begun to lead with my dick, and I *hate* those guys.

Jessie opens my office door, she looks pale and still a little green around the gills. "I wanted to come in for a few hours this afternoon, where should I start?"

"You should start by sitting down. You look like a strong breeze could knock you over," I say as I point to the other office chair. "And secondly, you missed this afternoon by a couple of hours, it's almost five o'clock."

"I know, I didn't want to leave you hanging though," she says as she flops down in the chair.

"Well, it's a good thing you came in for these last eleven minutes then," I say from between the dual monitors on my desk.

"I also want to do this," she says as she slides a box across my desk.

"A pregnancy test?"

"I'm not so sure I have the flu."

"I mean, why would you?" I say sarcastically, "When so many of the people you have been spending time with all have it? Plus, you should be doing this with Silas," I say as I point to the box.

"Even if it says I am pregnant, I would want to be sure, so I would take another one anyway, I can do that one with him."

"And you're sure you want to have this moment with me?" I'm skeptical, but also doubtful she really is pregnant.

"Yes! Salinger, you were the first one to be supportive of me doing this for Devin and Corey. The first one. So yes, I want to have this moment with you."

"Ok, well, I can't pee on the stick for you," I say as I motion for her to hurry up. I still have to eat and walk Nash before going to the club tonight.

While she is in the restroom, I close down the program on my computer and tidy up my desk.

She comes in holding the stick and then sets the urine soaked thing right on my desk while she unfolds the directions.

"Two lines means you're pregnant, one line means you did the test right, but you're not pregnant," I say flatly.

"Wow, so knowledgeable about pregnancy tests. Are you sure you don't have a couple little Salingers running around?" The comment is meant to be funny, but I feel it sharply in my soul. To camouflage the unguarded look on my face, I grab the stick, but not by the peed on end even though it *is* covered by a plastic cap.

"It takes three minutes, I don't think it's been long enough yet," she says while nervously twirling a lock of red hair around her finger.

"JB, you are pregnant," I say. I'm certain there are two lines, not one dark one and one light one, two very distinct lines. I stand up and walk around my desk to give her a hug. I can feel her shaking in my arms. This is not the way I would have liked to take a pregnancy test with Jessie. My version would be that she is engaged to me, and expecting my baby, so I'm glad she doesn't know what to say, it gives me a second to compose myself.

"Congratulations, Jessie! This is very exciting!" I manage to get out.

She is crying, and I don't sense that they are happy tears, so I pull back a little to look her in the eyes. "You probably feel very overwhelmed right now, and that's perfectly normal. It's ok to be scared, Jessie." Then all I can do is hold her against me, the woman I can never have and the baby that is not mine.

"Salinger, am I doing the right thing? All of a sudden I'm having second thoughts," then she breaks down sobbing. I hold her tighter. Her arms are clamped around me too.

"You are absolutely doing the right thing, Honey. This is exactly how you are supposed to feel right now. You wouldn't be normal if you didn't have all these feelings crop up, I promise."

"I mean, I am happy, this is what I wanted, right?"

"Jessie, it's easy to think about something abstractly and feel ready for something like this. It's different once the abstract becomes real. You are still just as ready as before, but now you have to get used to it being real and not a hypothetical idea anymore. It's a natural adjustment, Sweetheart," I wipe her tears and wish I could say something profound that would actually make her feel better.

"Thank you, Salinger. I love you so much."

"I know, JB. I love you too."

Chapter Eleven

Bradley

Every time I start feeling better about being able to let my heart out of its concrete confinement, something happens that sends me running back to the club to remind myself I don't need that sappy, fucking heart. Today it was Jessie telling me she loves me. I know she meant it like she loves me as her friend, and that she loves that I'm always there for her, but still, those words from her mouth and directed at me, hit me like a battle ax.

Jessie is pregnant. Now I can watch her swell with life as the outsider I am. Good old, reliable Salinger, always there when you need a pick-me-up, but always on the wrong side of the glass. This is why the club is good for me. I need its constant reminders that I am desirable. That I actually add a modicum of value to the world.

Well, first just let me tamp down all my useless emotions, and then I'll go where I feel important, and people actually crave time with me. It's intoxicating really, to be so highly sought after. I needn't have worried about a cleansing period before embarking on a relationship with Avery, it has never been more clear to me that I am not ready for a relationship.

Between my devastation about Silas and Jessie, and feeling like my cock is all I've got worth offering someone, Avery would get caught in the crosshairs. She wouldn't even see it coming, the hollow, shell of a man that she takes for well adjusted.

Avery is different, I can't do that to her. I need to cancel paintball on Saturday. But now I'm off to fuck Bradley for all the voyeurs, in a place where I feel welcome and wanted.

***

We meet at the bar, Bradley and I. She is my perfect counterpart because she is valued for her body, her arms are covered in tattoos like mine, and we are both irreparably damaged. She is beautiful though, and if all I'm going to care about are surface relationships, this is a good one. Bradley and I are like Gladiators in the arena of 1462, in that we are good for the show. Only, instead of fighting lions and other warriors, we fight ourselves, quietly. It's an equal bloodbath and the carnage is similar, except Bradley's and mine is on the inside.

"What are you thinking about? You seem so stoic tonight," Bradley says, while she swirls her gin & tonic in the glass. Does she actually want me to open up to her? That would be a sprint in the opposite direction of our mutual alliance.

"I'm fine, there is just a lot going on at work," I answer, already surmising that she isn't interested in what I have to say anyway. Actually, maybe she is interested, she did ask in the first place, and we need to start somewhere.

"Sounds like you need to clear your head," she says with a mischievous grin on her face. She slides off the barstool, and her hand goes immediately to my dick. Then I have to recalibrate again, of course, she does not want me to open up to her. Why would she? It's not like I'm a real person behind this hard cock or anything.

"I want you to fuck me in the peeping Tom shower, I've already posted that's where we'll be, so I know we will have a bunch of viewers," she says as she clamps down her hand, tighter than I'm entirely comfortable with, and disregarding the fact that there is a zipper between her palm and my commando penis.

"Lead the way, I was just thinking I could use a third shower today," I say, while she presses her body up against me. She misses my sarcasm but not my stiffening penis.

"I can't wait to feel your fat cock inside my wet cunt. I've been fantasizing about it for days."

"Bradley, you're so romantic. You really know how to woo a man, you know that?"

"Your cock bursting in my pussy is all the romance I need, Salinger," she smiles then bites down on my bottom lip.

"Got it," I say. Her crude statement just reaffirms where I should be placing my value—as if that was ever in question.

***

The peeping Tom shower is really more of a locker room, with peeper holes everywhere and a big, multi-faucet shower out in the open. I don't particularly get off knowing we are being watched, but I'm past the point of feeling self-conscious about it.

Bradley takes off her jacket and her jeans right away and is left in satin panties and a cutoff football jersey. The jersey *just* covers her nipples when her arms are down, and she looks sexy as fuck. Now I'm all done feeling sorry for myself.

I close in and kiss her while she tugs my shirt, eventually pulling it over my head. Then she starts working on my jeans. I slide her panties down, turn her around, and then help her to raise one foot to the locker room bench while her hands are stretched forward to press against the lockers.

With one leg on either side of the bench, I sit behind her while she is in a bent forward position. Her pussy is right in front of me, so I lean forward to bury my face between her slippery, pink lips. I reach between her thighs to dally with her clit. I've learned that she doesn't like movement against her clit as much as constant pressure, so me toying with it is for my own enjoyment before I press into her body.

I'm a very perceptive lover, I pick up really quickly what works and what doesn't work. For Bradley, it's pressure rather than movement against her clit, for Mary-Jane, it's being spanked while being fucked, for my ex-wife, she liked her nipples pinched while I ate her out. Everyone has that one thing, you only need to listen.

"That's right, fuck my pussy with your tongue!" she cries out, probably more for the viewers than to direct me. I can feel her getting close, it's like there is a change in the muscles around her vagina, like tension I suppose. I press her clit harder against her, and she explodes in my mouth while screaming, "Oh fuck, Salinger, fuck, fuck!" I stay between her legs, but I back my tongue off about eighty percent. She gets so sensitive after she comes, anything more than gentle licks and swirls with my tongue is too much for her.

She stands, tugs my jeans down then off, and re-positions us so I'm lying back with my knees bent, and legs still on either side of the bench. She has me down on the end like this because while she blows me, she wants to lean over and display her glistening crotch to the peep-holes in the wall. Whenever she gives me head, she always stimulates my prostate by sticking her finger in my ass. It felt a little invasive at first, but I got right over it, it feels so fucking good.

The way her legs are spread and she is bent forward, the cutoff jersey falls away from her body and showcases her tits for everyone but me. I stop her from continuing my BJ, tell her to get a condom from my jeans pocket, and then settle her on my lap facing me.

This top she is wearing is even sexier than not wearing a top at all. The glimpses of her tits from just beneath the cut edge of the jersey are driving me wild. She rolls the condom on my rock hard cock, then reaches up to gather her blonde hair on top of her head. Of course, this action raises the bottom of the jersey, so it no longer conceals anything, and my hands go instantly to her tits.

She likes her nipples roughly pinched and tugged, not sucked on, which is just as well for me because I love pinching and tugging them while they are right in front of me like this. Seeing how her nipples respond to my treatment of them is so fucking erotic, so carnal.

"Get on my cock, Bradley," I command, and she does, sliding down it in slow motion while my dick burrows through her pussy's silky resistance. When she starts riding me, with her tits bouncing in front of my face, I have to grab her ass and slow her tempo, so I don't blow my wad right away.

She pushes me back against the bench again, and again it's so she can show off her pussy while it's being penetrated. The view for all the voyeurs is her pussy repeatedly swallowing my gleaming erection, and each calculated movement of hers is meant to maximize the amount of her ass hole and vagina that's visible to everyone.

"Do you like when I ride your cock like this? Nice and slow, with my tits in your face?" she asks, as if she can't tell.

Instead of answering her, I pose my own question, "Do you like having my cock stretch your pussy like this? Filling you up, and grinding against your g-spot?" The dirty talk, coupled with my thick penis makes her come again, this time in clenching waves while she falls against my chest, moaning loudly with each quake and spasm of her vaginal walls. Seeing her reaction, and knowing I did that to her, is enough for me to let go into the tight clutch of her vagina.

"Salinger," she whispers, "I want you to finger me in the shower, right in front of the big peep-hole." Her choice to be fingered is not a sexual preference, it's simply so she can be properly spread open without having my pesky body blocking the view any more than is absolutely necessary.

I honestly don't think this chick could get off if she wasn't being watched. She is a natural performer, even worked in a circus type show in Vegas for a long time, but her desire to intimately show herself to people is problematic. Her need is growing, and it's getting harder for her to chase a fix. It used to be enough for her to strip in nightclubs, then it escalated to extra special lap dances, now, she goes dogging to let strangers grope and fondle her because it's such a rush to have someone unknown touch her.

I think her predilections started with wanting people to *see* her, you know, opening her legs in a restaurant without any panties on, having her shirt accidentally fall open, stuff like that. But this desire to be seen has morphed into a need to be *used*, like letting a stranger approach her in the car and finger her while she lays herself open for whomever. I worry about her after I stop coming to the club, and yes, someday I will stop coming to the club. I worry about the lengths she will continue to go to.

In the meantime, I'm only serving to enable her escalating behavior. I'm not even sure if I should be relieved she has someone like me to fuck, or if I should feel wretched because I'm sanctioning her destructive habits. Either way, I'm going to go finger her in front of her adoring fans, then go home feeling just as empty as I did before.

Chapter Twelve

Mary-Jane

This place is fast becoming my second home, and I feel like I've embraced that I'm this guy now. I have no business going out with Avery on Saturday. I will ruin any spark before it's even been lit. I know that. My relationship views have been so drastically skewed, I'm afraid of starting something that could be real.

A relationship with Avery would be doomed from the start because what normal, healthy woman wants someone who has had his dick in four different chicks just this week? Because let's not forget that tomorrow night will not just be one woman, it will be two, plus a dude...and then throw in anal sex with Rebecca, and all hopes of a normal relationship with Avery go down in flames.

I had meant to cancel our double date this afternoon but got so buried with work shit, that it honestly slipped my mind. Then I was going to do it when I took Nash out, but I was in such a hurry to get here to meet Mary-Jane. Tomorrow is already Thursday; I have to do it tomorrow. My first priority when I get to work will be to cancel the date. I can't just say something came up either because then I'd have to reschedule. I'm going to have to level with them and say I'm not at a point in my life where I want to date. God, I sound like a dick. Even hearing it in my own head makes me want to punch myself. So, tomorrow morning it is. Now, I have to go meet Mary-Jane at the bar.

"Hi, Beautiful," I say as I sit down. The club is busy tonight for a Wednesday. The main room has been set up like the dungeon rooms, except out in the open. There must be some sort of demonstration going on tonight.

"Hey, Baby!" She tosses her long black hair over her shoulder as she turns to me. I lean in and kiss her because I'm not a total savage. Her lips taste like bubble gum, and it makes me want to suck on them.

"What's going on out here tonight?" I ask.

"A fire demonstration, and then your standard BDSM stuff. Do you have some time tonight, I've been hearing all about the demonstration, and I'd love to watch it."

"Absolutely, I have all the time in the world for you tonight," I smile and mean it too. Mary-Jane is a beautiful, amazing woman. She is going through some of her own shit right now. She is recently divorced, and from what I can gather, her ex-husband really kept her under his thumb. He was very controlling and supremely jealous, so I think the club is more of a cleanse for her. My guess is that she will ultimately transition through this phase and settle down with someone who is kind to her. She also has a daughter, who she is fighting to get full custody of. Mary-Jane is a normal, everyday woman that you would see at the gym and never guess where she spends her free time.

For the most part, those are the kind of people you find at 1462, everyday folks who like a little adventure drizzled on their sex life. However, there are those who legitimately want to dominate someone and those who are into the whole submissive thing. They represent a healthy percentage of members too. Actually, it looks like we will be seeing a few of them tonight if the set-up is any indication.

I get the psychology behind wanting to be a submissive. You know, the dude who is in control of everything all day long and just wants to relinquish power and be tended to for a change. I understand the desire, but I can't bring myself to find that quality in a person attractive. Then, there is the mindset of the Doms. I guess, similar to the subs, it probably has something to do with feeling weak in mainstream life, or their perception of everything being out of control, and wanting to regulate that which can be controlled. All those people are fine for me as long as everything is perfectly consensual.

The club goers who remain a complete mystery to me are the ones who want to cause pain to someone else. Not just a pinch or ass slap either, I'm referring to the ones wielding the whips and floggers in a not-so-sexy way. I've seen a woman bound to a St. Andrew's cross and flogged to the point her whole body was shaking. The entire back half of her body was angry red, and you could see the agony plainly on her face…but she liked it. She told me later, it causes a release of tension so supreme that she feels a sense of elation after, even feels rapturous. To me, that feeling is owing to the massive pain endorphins released, but whatever.

The ones who make my skin crawl are the guys who want to severely hurt and actually *harm* someone. I've seen some sexy knife play where there was no cutting, and it was more for sensation purposes, much like lightly dragging a fingernail across someone's skin. But I've also seen someone draw blood before, and there was nothing sexy about it. In fairness, he was kicked out of the club, and they brought in some sort of hazmat team to address the blood, but still.

"Salinger, what's wrong, you've hardly touched your drink?" Mary-Jane asks.

"Nothing's wrong. I'm happy to be here with you," I smile, perhaps with less enthusiasm than I would have liked.

"Oh look, I think they are about to get started," she says excitedly. It would take so little to make this woman happy. Someone who is gentle and kind is all it would take. It makes me angry about her ex-husband. How could he have treated her so badly?

The lights dim almost down to nothing at all. A man walks out in a black kilt, and black boots. He is bare-chested and looks like a fierce Norseman. His hair is long and scraggly but held back with a leather tie. He takes a moment to check his supply table and then asks in a booming voice if he has any volunteers. Uhh, nope.

A handful of women raise their hands, and he chooses one of them to join him. He tells her to undress and lie face down on the table. She must have been planning for this because she lifts her dress over her head and is completely naked underneath.

"Good thing she has short hair," I say to Mary-Jane as she wraps her arms around my bicep and leans into me. I kiss her temple, she deserves so much more than me.

The Kilt guy raises what looks to me like two skewers with large marshmallows on the ends, and then lights them on fire. He starts swinging them around in a theatrical manner, so I feel more like I'm at a Hawaiian luau than a fire play show at a BDSM club. That is, until he blows one out, drags his hand up the volunteer's leg, across her butt, and down the other leg. Then lights her on fire with the still lit marshmallow skewer.

Mary-Jane gasps as we watch the blue flame follow the reverse path of the one his hand just took. As the flame slowly burns out, he swipes his palm over the fire trail. Then he does it again and again, each time creating a new path with his palm, lighting it, and then following the flame with his hand.

His model arches her back and pushes her ass up as if the sensation is intensely itchy. Hearing the cheers of the crowd, she puts on even more of a show and starts bringing her high heeled feet alternately back to her butt, then back down. As icy looking, blue flames crawl all over her body, she cranes her back like a stretching cat, then begins slowly waving her ass back and forth in a way that tells me she was not randomly chosen as a volunteer. Her body movements can be best described as a slow, erotic, writhe. Again, it's like the whole thing tickles like crazy.

The fire presentation doesn't look like it's hurting the women, but judging by the faint smell of singed hair, the flame is evidently burning something. The demonstration goes on for about thirty minutes before he winds up for what I can only assume is the grand finale. He sprays a foamy, white substance from a can on her, and then creates a fairly elaborate design crisscrossing her back and legs. When he lights the end of the foam, the flame snakes across her naked body, sometimes even branching into two flames that cross over each other.

"Oh my goodness! That was so cool!" Mary-Jane says, with her eyes wide, and genuinely impressed.

"That *was* cool. I always thought fire play was on the more sadomasochistic side of BDSM, but not at all. Don't you think it was more artistic than anything?" I ask as she nods in complete agreement.

Now that the show is over, a group of people have approached the Nordic dude with questions. He sprays the foam on a few of their arms, then lights it to allow them to see what it feels like.

"What do you want to do now?" I ask Mary-Jane. "Don't tell me you want me to wear a kilt and light you on fire though because I'm all out of foam and marshmallows."

She giggles then takes a dainty sip of her vodka and cranberry juice. "I'd like to sit here with you for a while," she actually blushes, "We can watch the D/s crowd for a bit, then, if you want to we can go to a room."

If I want to? She is trying to be so accommodating to me. I get glimpses now and then of how her husband has broken her spirit, and it makes me want to track him down and beat his ass.

"Mary-Jane, I would love to sit here with you for a while, and then if *you* want to, we can go to a room," I say, and the way she looks at me makes me feel like I'm the first guy to ever care about what she wants.

"Have you ever been bound to anything like that stuff?" she asks, indicating all the bondage contraptions next to the bar area in the main room of the club.

"No. I'm not sure I would like being held down," I answer, "I'm that guy that gets squirrely if a jacket is too tight. I have to be able to move, or I start to feel trapped."

"I think being trapped is part of the allure for some people," she says.

"I think I would panic, and wig out," I say, and I'm completely serious. I can literally not think of anything that would give me more of a compulsion to move, than being forcibly held down, or bound to something.

"What about you? I know you like to be spanked, what about bound?" I ask as I look around at the equipment. People are already making themselves at home with the stuff. One guy catches my eye because the lady with him looks like a battered woman. Not beat up and bruised or anything, just, you know? Beat down. I bet this chump treats her like Mary-Jane's husband treated her.

"I do like it, I like the loss of control," she says. I hope she doesn't want to go to a bondage room tonight because I'm not the guy to flog or cane her. I want to ask her if a man has ever made love to her before, but I'm afraid it would give her the wrong impression. So I change tactics.

"Tell me about your daughter," I say as I signal the bartender for another round.

***

For the last hour, while engaged in witty conversation with Mary-Jane, I've watched this douche bag mistreat the woman he's with. First, he had her over a spanking bench, where he paddled her ass for forty-five minutes, then, he told her to get up and go over to the padded table where he cuffed her ankles and wrists to each corner, leaving her spread eagle for the crowd. That evolution in itself isn't what bothers me, it's watching her go through the motions. She looks like a baby bird with two broken wings. She can hardly walk after being paddled so hard and for *so* long. She is completely downtrodden, her shoulders are hunched forward, and she has yet to take her eyes off the floor. This is an abusive relationship, and this guy is going to get his ass kicked.

"Salinger, I think it's part of the whole role play. It's their thing," Mary-Jane says in an attempt to get me to put my hackles down.

"I don't think so. Did you see how meek she was when she walked over to the table? She is *not* enjoying this, and someone needs to teach that cocksucker a lesson." I get up from the barstool and Mary-Jane grabs my arm.

"Salinger, don't."

"Let's just go stand over there a little closer. I need to get a better read on this situation," is what I say, but I already have all the information I need. This fucker is going to see what it's like to get beat down. She slides off her stool as well and walks a little closer with me, but she isn't done trying to change my mind.

"Really, it's the whole Dom/sub thing... some people get really into it. Plus, the moderators would stop it if he was crossing the line."

"Then why aren't they? I can see four of them from here," I point out, wondering what the hell they are even for if they won't stop something like this.

Now that I'm closer to the situation, my rage is building, and I feel like I will put him in the hospital if he gives me the slightest provocation.

He is whipping her naked, spread open thighs like a lion tamer because he's standing way back and letting the crack of the whip lick at the same spot on her inner thigh over and over. The spot is red and inflamed, and I can almost feel the burn of it. Once he finally moves from that spot, it only gets worse because he begins bringing the sting of the whip right down against her bare vagina. The pain must be so intense against that tender skin, I cringe with each snap. The woman is whimpering and crying, so I've seen all I need to.

As I charge toward that smug motherfucker, two moderators grab my arms and haul me to a stop. I struggle with them trying to free myself, "Oh, I see how this goes. You're going to try to stop *me*, while that piece of shit abuses the fuck out of her?!" Now I'm really battling to free myself, I'm putting up a good fight too because both moderators are out of breath.

"It's not like that. Stop! Will you just hold still? Goddamnit, listen to me!" the guy on my right shouts.

"Get your fucking hands off of me! Nothing you have to say interests me. How can you two pussies stand here and watch that go on?!"

"Stop struggling and listen to me!" guy on my right, again.

"Bro, we're trying to help you!" guy on my left.

"You two pussies couldn't help yourselves off a ladder!"

"I know it looks bad," guy on my right.

"Trust us, we know," guy on my left, "That's why we were ready for you."

"What the fuck are you talking about!?" I'm almost curious why they *were* on me like flies on shit.

"Trust me, we have all talked to her."

"And to him."

"She is very much a willing participant. Will you stop fighting for a minute and let me explain? Fuck!" guy on the right.

"Ok," I stop struggling, but neither of them let up their hold on me. They must know if they do, they will both get decked.

The guy on my right, "We have been through this a million times with them. We've talked to her privately, the whole nine yards. She likes this treatment, she wants it to go down like this."

"Bro, you're not even the first one who has tried to step in."

"Are you kidding me? This is a joke right?" I'm still really fired up, but they seem to genuinely understand my state of mind.

"Buddy, I *promise* you, this would not happen under our noses if it was shady at all."

"Dude, you can ask her yourself once their little scene is over." They must feel me calm down a little because they both loosen their grip on my arms.

"Are you being completely serious right now? She isn't just saying what he expects her to?"

"Yes. This is very gallant of you, but yes, it's completely consensual." Now they release me altogether.

"We just saved your membership, Buddy," guy on my left.

"I have to say, I do like where your heart's at. What's your name?" the guy on my right asks.

"Salinger."

"Salinger, you're a good man, but something like that will get your membership revoked if you're not careful."

"I'd still like to pop that motherfucker in the jaw," I say as I adjust my shirt.

"There are a lot of guys in here that agree with you. I'm Paul, by the way."

Mary-Jane sees that tempers have cooled and comes over to tuck herself under my arm. I guess to show her delayed support? Or maybe to gloat?

"Were you really waiting for me to make my move?" I ask.

"Yeah, for the last twenty minutes. Did you happen to see how we all shifted our positions?" Paul laughs.

"Each one of us recognized that look on your face, and then eased on over here," the other guy says with amusement.

"Salinger, let's go to a room," Mary-Jane says, and I can almost feel the lust radiating from her body.

My surging pulse has mostly calmed down, so with one last look at that piece of shit with the whip, I turn to follow her lead. I'm not saying I won't still beat the shit out of that guy, I just won't do it right now.

Chapter Thirteen

Toll

It's Thursday night, and when I get home from the club, I fall face first onto my bed. I'm actually drained, physically and sexually. The amount of energy exerted during a group sex session is remarkable. I feel like every drop of cum has been milked from my body along with any that my balls will manufacture in the next month.

This week has taken a toll on me mentally as well. I've had sex with four different people in the last three days, actually five because to some extent I had sex with Carter, you know, by proxy. The fact that I have become a straight-up manwhore has exerted a heavy toll as well. Mostly because, I'm not that guy, or I didn't used to be anyway, I am now, clearly.

It makes me feel cheap and dirty, kind of unfit for normal life outside of the club. I always have this sense of buyer's remorse when I'm no longer caught in the seductive grip of 1462. But, God knows, I'm all-in when I'm there. This is the biggest reason I can't go out with anyone right n— FUCK! I forgot to cancel the double date! Shit! I turn to look at the clock, it's eleven forty-seven, I sure as fuck can't call them now.

Tomorrow morning will be fine if I do it right away. I'll do it first thing. As an afterthought, I slide my shoes off with the help of the opposite foot, but I can't get up to take out my contacts or brush my teeth, I'm way too tired.

Chapter Fourteen

Lemons

"JB, what the hell are you doing?" I ask Jessie as she rings each fingertip, one by one in a cut lemon. I'm standing in the doorway of her office, looking kind of disgusted if you want to know the truth.

"It helps with the nausea," she says. She looks like she has been rode hard and put away wet. There are dark circles under her eyes, and her face is pale, more pale than normal anyway.

"Is that an old wives tale or something? How can lemon juice on your fingertips help with nausea?" I ask, the whole thing sounds pretty kooky if you ask me. Instead of answering, she raises her hand and puts a finger in her mouth.

"Oooooo, right. Got it," I say stupidly. Seeing her suck on her finger would be totally hot if she didn't look like a walking plague victim.

"It's bad, Salinger, the morning sickness is round the clock. I can't possibly nourish a fetus if I can't even keep a sip of water down," she looks pained.

"The *baby* will take what he or she needs. You just need to look after yourself right now. Have you tried popsicles?"

"Popsicles?" she says, as if I just suggested she commit a class three felony.

"Yes."

91

"Actually, a popsicle does sound kind of good right now," she says, then scrunches up her face in earnest contemplation, "Do adults even eat popsicles?"

"JB, a little hydration wouldn't kill you."

She quickly shoves a different finger into her mouth, briefly looks up at me with horror, then leans forward and barfs in her lap. I give her a bit before I suggest perhaps she find a toilet. She shakes her head and holds up a finger, as if telling me she will be right with me.

"Trashcan," she whispers as she looks up. She drags the back of her hand across her mouth. The motion would be sexy if she were backing off a blowjob instead of wiping gastric acid off her blanched lips.

"You need a trash can?" I ask, wondering whose office I could swipe one from that wouldn't notice.

"No, I have a trash can down here. I would never make it to the toilet unless I was already in there peeing."

"Well then, my work here is done," I say as I start to back out of her office.

"Salinger?" *Damn it, so close.*

"Yeah?"

She doesn't answer, but she does treat me to another bout of what is essentially a cat hacking on a hairball.

"Sit tight, JB. I'll take care of this," I say, and this time I double-time it out of her office before she can compel me to stay and hold witness to her gastric atrocities.

I was thinking I would get out of the office a little early today, but acknowledging my designation to the friend zone, I grab my jacket instead.

***

Once I return from the grocery store, I half expect Jessie to have thrown in the towel and gone home. But, as luck would have it, she is still here, tapping lemon tipped fingers all over her keyboard.

"Are you feeling a little better?" I ask, as if the gaunt look on her face doesn't tell me all I need to know. I put the bag down on her desk then sit down, facing her.

"In a word, no."

"Ok, start here," I say as I open the box of popsicles and hand her one. She takes it with a shaky hand.

"You went and got me all this stuff?" she asks, her voice cracking as if I just donated a kidney instead of going to the corner store.

"It was a purely selfish good deed because I need you to pick up your own weight and drag it across the finish line," I'm trying to be light, but the truth is I would have braved a zombie apocalypse if it would help her start feeling better.

"You are more than I deserve, Salinger. Thank you."

"Ok, there are crackers that will help soak up the churning stomach acid, broth, Vitamin Water, squeeze-y lemon juice, and a variety of popsicles—not the crappy kind full of high fructose corn syrup either." When I look up from the bounty, she is sitting back in her chair with a juice popsicle in her mouth and her eyes closed.

"JB?" I prompt. She opens her eyes and looks at me. "Are you gonna make it?"

She nods, "I think so."

"Ok, go a little easy here though, give the popsicle ten or fifteen then have a couple of crackers, maybe a sip of Vitamin Water."

"I can feel the effects of the popsicle already," she says, closing her eyes again. "I don't even feel like barfing it back up."

"Well, there's still time," I say, with a sardonic smile on my face that she can't even see. "I'm going to take the popsicles to the break room freezer. I'll check on you in a while, and bring you some warm broth," I say. The truth is, I'm a little disappointed in Silas, Devin, and Corey. Between the three of them, I'd have thought they would have enough sense to make sure she had these basic items on hand.

Whatever, I'll do her job, my job, and their jobs too because hey, that's just the kind of doormat I am. On that note, I better get back to my desk because someone needs to keep this ship afloat.

93

Chapter Fifteen

Nash

By the time I get home Nash is about to pee himself, so he charges past me with no concern for the fact that I haven't even grabbed his leash, let alone that I didn't go out the door first. I guess I would rather him disregard my alpha status for a moment than have to clean up the lake of pee he would have left instead. I have considered a dog door to the backyard, but he is so big and uncoordinated. First off, it would have to be huge—like, man-sized, and second of all, I'm not too sure he could get his long, gangly limbs through the flap. He is definitely formidable, but graceful he is not. For that matter, if a circus of burglars came through the dog door, Nash would welcome them like they were the Queen of England instead of hell-bent on divesting me of my high-end electronics.

"You done, Dude?" I ask him as I raise my arms in question. He has the sense to look at least a little ashamed to have nearly plowed me over. Then he trots back inside to commence with the pesky formalities of our normal routine.

It's Friday night, and I'm actually jonesing to go to the club. I highly doubt Jessie and Silas will be anywhere near 1462, but I'm going to stick to my rules and steer clear of it on weekends. Friday and Saturday nights have more of a raging party feel anyway, and always have themes. Tonight is a masquerade ball for those who like playing dress-up as grown adults.

I myself, will be getting acquainted with my couch and maybe giving my dick a rest. Today was insanely busy at work because Jessie was mostly dead-weight, but I'll always cover for her because she helped me limp along after my chaotic return to civilian life. Without her help picking up my slack for all those months, I would have been shit-canned for sure.

It's not until the end of Nash's walk when I'm reflecting on the fact the runners—I always refer to the two women as *the runners*, even though we encounter many other runners as well—always seem to find their way to where I am. It's an innate ability they have or something. They don't even run together, although they must know each other by this point.

Our walks are completely inconsistent, early, late, over to the dog park, along the creek, whatever. They always somehow catch up to us. If they knew what a shit bag I was they wouldn't bother. It seems I have the sexual appetite of a frat boy, and the same path of destruction as an unguided missile. If you would have told me a few months ago that I would be chewing up and spitting out women like I am, I would have broken your jaw, and yet here I am.

I stop walking. Nash looks up at me, and then politely sits down to wait for my epiphany moment to pass.

"Holy shit, Nash! I never canceled the fucking date for tomorrow!" The way he cocks his head makes me think he is astounded by my degenerate memory and would call me a dumb ass if he could.

"I actually have to go through with this," I say out loud. I have to suck it up and present myself as a normal guy. A guy who doesn't call a sex club his second home, and fuck upwards of five different people a week. What a disaster.

It's going to go against every noble fiber in my being, but I will have to come off as either uninterested or as a complete douche bag, so Avery loses interest in me. I'm serious about needing a cool-down phase before I try to mingle with polite society. I just wish I would have remembered to take care of this shit days ago. Great, now I'm in a shitty mood.

Chapter Sixteen

Paint

The paintball place is outdoors, in a wooded area sprinkled with various bunker items to use as cover. Quite a few people are milling around waiting for the next round to begin. I see lots of camouflage as well as full-blown paintball getups with chest protection, and knee and elbow pads built right in. As for me, I wore jeans with a black hoodie and baseball cap and even left my jacket in the car.

I see Avery and the guys standing over by the gear shop, so I head over there. I've made sure to arrive no less than twenty minutes late, and then offer no apology though one sits heavy in my mouth. They are all standing around chatting, and none of them bat an eyelash at my late arrival. After my quick greeting and barely a glance at Avery, Corey suggests we head in to fill out our paperwork.

We end up getting rushed through the formalities because, due to my late arrival, we only have about fifteen minutes to sign waivers, choose our markers; which is paintballer language for guns, gear up, and listen to a hasty delivery of the rules.

In a nutshell, the rules are don't lift your goggles/mask ever, even to wipe off paint, keep the barrel cover and safety on while in the staging area, and when you get hit, raise your hands and yell "Hit" then walk off the field until the next round.

The markers are pretty basic—nothing like an M-16, they have a small compressed air tank on the back, a hopper on the top, and the barrel is nothing more than a pretentious looking pipe. The goggles are like ski goggles with a plastic face guard and foam ear covers, some have visors, some don't. I happen to know my glasses will fog up under the goggles, so I've already taken the liberty of spraying them with anti-fog spray.

Some of these guys out here even have full tactical belts with extra pods of paintballs. I'm told the hopper holds two hundred of them, so that should be plenty for me to clear the field. As legit as some of these guys look, I doubt most of them have ever seen any actual combat.

I'm happy to see Devin, Corey, and Avery are dressed much like me, nothing showy. Avery is wearing a mossy green bandanna around the top of her head and two loose braids on the sides. In the interest of full disclosure, her eyes are piercing, and they look the exact same color as the bandanna. Right off, two things impress me about her. One, she is naturally beautiful without having to be all done up, and two, she could not care less about how rude I am being to her.

"I'm going to run to the bathroom real quick before we get started," Avery says.

"I'll walk over there with you, I need to go too," Corey says as he shuffles along beside her.

When they are gone, Devin wastes no time, "Salinger! What are you doing?"

"What are you talking about?" I ask as I turn my hat around backward.

"You know exactly what I'm talking about! You're being such a dick!" he hisses.

Saving me from having to play dumb any longer, a referee comes over and hands us two blue armbands. "Put these on your left arm, once we start, you'll have five minutes to strategize with your team over by the blue map."

"Got it," I say, and wonder if Corey and Avery will end up on our same team.

As luck would have it, and to my complete relief, they do not end up on our team. Perfect, that cuts down on our interaction and saves me from this whole asshole routine for a little while.

When we gather with the team, which is roughly twenty of us, a couple guys immediately take over delegating our plan of attack. They assign jobs and determine who is to go where. I'm tasked with making my way up the top side field and clearing the back line while these two mavericks sweep the bottom side and go for the flag. Pretty much everyone else is to provide cover in one form or another and try to flank the other team. The basic strategy is good, but I modify it slightly when I tell Devin to stay with me instead of his designated, easily picked off position in the inside sector.

I have every intention of clearing this field down to Corey and Avery, and me and Devin, which is when the real fun will begin. I happen to know that Corey will be doing the same thing, even though I didn't talk to him after the teams were split up.

The first thing I need to do is get a few shots off and figure out how this thing fires and the arc of the paintball, I can make any necessary calibrations after that on the fly.

"Devin, listen to me. Don't post-up over the top of something, your hopper is the first thing some of these seasoned players will look for."

"Got it," he says with a quick nod.

"Also, keep your gu..I mean your marker up, even if you are about to run, if it's up and someone sees you, they don't know if you are going to run or shoot. If it's down, they don't have to worry about you shooting them, they know you are going to run. Easy pickings."

"Would you be disappointed in me if I told you I've never shot a gun?" Devin asks.

"No, of course not. Just hold the marker centered and level with your nose, and don't forget to hit the safety with your pointer. After we start, make sure to keep moving, and feather your fingers against the trigger, like this," I raise my hand and jiggle my middle finger and pointer quickly back and forth. "There are bunkers all over this field, and the trees provide great cover.

"Everyone, get to your starting point by your flag, on my air-horn, you begin," one of the referees shouts.

"My heart is already pounding, and this is just paint," Devin quips.
"Devin?"
"Yeah?"
"Don't get hit." Then the air-horn sounds and everyone scatters to their respective sectors and bunkers.

***

I have taken great joy in picking off the hot shots on the other team. I've been mostly leaving the others alone, and I have yet to see Corey or Avery. My favorite shot has been right in the T-box, which covers their goggles with paint and when placed dead center, it requires a certain walk of shame off the field. I know with near certainty, the T-box shots to our team have been delivered by Corey, with the same degree of show-off as me. Devin is holding his own, I only had to pull him back from his cover on the outside lane of a tree once before he realized he needed to stay on the inside lane to avoid being seen.

"Come on, we need to keep moving," I whisper to Devin. Once we hit our next batch of cover, in this case, a giant wooden spool formerly used to wind up underground cables, Devin asks, "How the fuck did you guys do this in real life?"

"Shh, listen to the pops back there. Someone is trying to flank us, follow me," I mouth more than anything.

As we get closer to the other team's base, and heavily guarded flag, I'm seeing their snipers, or at least their sniper's hoppers. The snipers might feel safer by not running around but my team is closing in on them, and it's getting harder and harder for them to hold their ground. Devin rolls out, fires three quick shots then pops back behind our bunker.

"Got another one," he says.

I can always tell when someone is about to run from their bunker because they get in a running stance and put their marker down. They are always easy to pick off, because I know they are not going to shoot back at me, just like I told Devin from the start.

I feel like the teams are taking comparable casualties, so now I need to actively target their weaker players. With them, I have not taken the shot more often than I have taken it because I want them to have fun and not head immediately to the sidelines. But now everyone is fair game. I hit three of their newbie snipers, and Devin covers our back, taking out one of the other team's hotshots sneaking up behind us.

"Let's go," I wave for him to follow me and we take off back into the trees. I'm not surprised I haven't seen Corey or Avery, but as time goes on, I'm increasingly worried about them. If I had to guess, I would say each team is probably down to four or five players by now.

"Fuck!" Devin says as he raises his hands and yells "Hit." Then I take off because someone obviously has eyes on us. While running for cover, I shoot it out with a red team player and get them in the shoulder before I dive behind some barrels. Judging by the angle of Devin's shoulder hit, that was the guy that shot him.

I have no way of knowing how many people are left, the game goes until one team captures the other team's flag or until one whole team is wiped out. I slow my breathing and listen for movement. I hear the tiniest rustle in the trees and spin around but don't see anyone. I do however feel vulnerable here, so I have to keep moving. I don't head straight toward the flag because that's what they expect. Instead, I drop in and come up behind it. Then I see Corey. He's in the thicket of trees about a hundred yards away. He has eyes on me, and I've spotted him, but the fact of the matter is that I don't think a paintball marker can hit someone at that distance.

He knows I'm close to their flag and I suspect he also has figured out the range of a paintball, so he has to make a move. He has to get in closer to me without getting shot once he's in range. The fact he isn't doing this faster makes me aware of a possible ambush. I turn to glass behind me, then quickly back to Corey. He's made a move, but I don't know where yet. When I spot the barrel of the marker, I take a shot just to the left, which is where he will have to pop out from. He's lucky because I would have hit him if he had moved just then. After another quick glance behind me, I fire to the right of Corey's barrel again, only this time nothing happens. I brush the trigger again. Nothing. Shit, I'm out of ammo. And to think I had laughed at the guys with full tactical belts and extra pod packs.

I have to think fast, and I can't let on that I'm out of paintballs. Now Corey makes his move and dives for cover. I would have had him, cleanly even, because I knew that was his next move. The red flag is a bit hidden, but it's less than twenty yards away from me. I have to go for it, because every second I wait, gives red the opportunity to close in on me. There is only a small cylinder of corrugated metal for cover between me and the flag, but I have to get there.

Then...I get hit, twice in quick succession. One hits me in the neck on my right side and stings like a bitch, and the second hit sprays yellow paint across my goggles from my right temple region. I swipe my forearm across my goggles then stand up just as the horn blares to life like an air raid siren. Shit, I was the last one. Game over.

I raise the goggles to the top of my head and see Corey and Avery strutting toward me with huge grins on their smug faces. I played right into their strategy, while Corey distracted me, Avery moved in.

They close in on me with high fives and general good cheer and despite my resolution not to, I smile and laugh with them.

Even though the blue team lost and I took a sharp hit to my pride with a paintball, this was the most fun I've had in a very long time. And damn it, the fact that Avery was one of the last two people on her team standing, is fucking sexy as hell.

Chapter Seventeen

Bar

After Avery got essentially two headshots on me and won the game for the red team, I was feeling less resistant to the whole date. So when Devin suggested we grab a bite to eat and have a few beers, I was all in.

We decided to meet at a local sports bar just so we could get all our cars back on this side of town. I didn't bring extra clothes, so it's a good thing the paintballs were filled with a gelatin-like substance that, for the most part, wipes off. There is, however, some bright yellow residue left on my hat, perhaps as a pompous reminder that Avery bested me on the field. Me, a MOS 0311!

We start with a pitcher of beer and a ridiculously huge plate of nachos. There are football games on all around us, plastered on huge screens and cheering fans to boot, but I'm not really interested in the games. Well, I might keep an eye on the scores, but not to the exclusion of my present company.

"Have you ever seen something so monstrously huge?" Devin asks, referring to the platter of nachos.

"I have," I respond, then start to chuckle, "Avery's ego!" Everyone laughs, and she rolls her green eyes at me. I think she's confused by me, because I was such a dick to start with, and now I'm playfully joking with her. Hell, I'm confused. On one hand, I want to warn her to stay far away from me, but on the other hand, I want to spread her out naked across these nachos and dip my face in her silky parts instead. I bet her pussy tastes like warm, ripe peaches, and with her brown hair and fair skin, I'm thinking her nipples are more tawny than pink. Heat starts to rush to my cock, trained as it is to perform lately. I'm glad my growing hard on is hidden by the table, because quite honestly it feels a little amateur.

"How did you manage to get the jump on Salinger anyway?" Devin asks.

"I'm sorry, I can't divulge strategic tactics, it's a matter of national security," she says with a completely aloof shrug. "But what I *can* tell you, is how satisfying it was to spray his goggles with a big yellow smear of paint."

"Yeah, and don't forget the one to my carotid artery. That was a particularly nice kill shot," I say before bringing the frosty mug to my lips.

"That must have hurt so bad!" Devin announces, "I got hit on the very outside of my arm, mostly sweatshirt in fact, but it still left a little sizzle by my shoulder."

"Avery and I wouldn't know what that feels like, would we, Avery?" Corey asks, basking in the camaraderie of their victory.

"I'll tell you exactly what it felt like, it felt like a close range rubber band snap, and if it leaves a bruise that looks like a hickey, someone is going down."

"Ooooooooo, tell us more," Devin says as he scoots forward on his stool and places his elbows on the table.

***

After a couple hours Devin and Corey start to wrap up their portion of the date, and I panic a little. I've begrudgingly had fun, but I haven't changed my mind about not being in the right head space to start seeing someone. Avery is great, which is the very reason a relationship wouldn't work out right now. I'm broken, and if it were just about

106

fucking her, I'd make room on the docket even though my dance card is more than full. But she is not the kind of girl you fuck at the club and then forget about until the next time you want to fuck her at the club. She's the kind of girl you want to know more about, the kind you want to wake up to every day.

I know enough about myself to know if I start dating her now, I will absolutely ruin it. Plain and simple, I can't have anything good in my life right now. And she would be good.

"Yeah, I better get going too, my dog has been inside all day," I say, and for a second it seems like the earth stops rotating. Everyone gets real still and quiet, which makes me freakishly-aware of Devin's silent gasp.

"Sounds good, I need to get home too. There is a pot I need to watch boil, or is it paint that's drying on the wall? I can never remember." Avery's snarky way of calling me out on my bullshit excuses is commendable. I like that she has a backbone and will stand up to me. Kind of reminds me of Jessie.

I'm not even out of the parking lot when my phone vibrates in my pocket. *Oh, here we go*, I cringe as I see the caller name displayed on my screen.

"Hi, Devin. Forget your to-go bag of nachos?" I ask, bracing myself for the fallout.

"You, Dumb Bitch, do you need Corey and I to stick your dick in her for you too?" It's less a reprimand than a slow, head shake of befuddlement.

"What makes you so sure I even want my dick in her?" I ask, trying not to smile at his contentiousness.

"Because, well—and this is an assumption on my part—but, because you *have* a dick," is his retort.

"Yeah, but that doesn't mean I want to shag every girl I see."

"She's not every girl. Avery can't even get the mail without giving someone a boner, and you pretend you're not interested? I mean, what the fuck?"

"Devin, since you've taken such a front row seat to my love life, I'm going to level with you."

"Please do."

"I can't date her right now. Did you know I fucked four (*five*) different people this week?" I say, hoping the shock of my statement will clamp down on any protective instinct he holds for Avery. He is like a brother to her, they grew up together. He should want to protect her from dirtbags like me, right?

"I mean…Should I alert the press? Or are you expecting some sort of medal?"

"Devin, I didn't just fuck them, I treated them like cum dumpsters. I used them and then threw them away." There, that should do it.

"*And?*"

"Devin, Jesus Christ, it wasn't just this week. It's been ever since I found out Jessie was engaged to Silas."

"Ok?" he says this as though he's still waiting for me to deliver my *actual* reason.

"Devin! I'm not in the right headspace, I think I'm still in love with Jessie, and I will walk all over a nice girl right now. The fact that I like you and Corey and Jessie is the very reason I need to keep *your friend*, Avery at arm's length. It may not be forever, but now is most assuredly not the right timing."

"I disagree."

"*Well, fuck!* I'm glad we got that cleared up," I laugh at this, because he won't let it go, he's so damn persistent.

"She's running away from something too, so it might not be a good time for her either."

"Ok then," *finally.*

"I think you guys could muddle through your crap together."

I shake my head but have no response to his assertiveness. When he remains quiet, I ask, "What's she running away from anyway?"

"Yeah, you should find that out," he says, the part he doesn't say out loud is, *Duh!*

"I'm hanging up now. You're not listening to me anyway, you pushy little fuck." He can hear the laughter in my voice but doesn't return it.

"Your loss, Champ."

Chapter Eighteen

Address

After getting home, I change and go straight to the basement. I need a good workout before spending the rest of the night on the couch watching the highlight reel on ESPN. Nash comes down with me, but I think it's only to express his disappointment in the form of forlorn looks and idle stares. Tonight I only work the heavy bag for about ten minutes and the speed bag for five. I want my focus on the free weights today, and besides, punishing my muscles feels good.

It's been over an hour. The music is loud and penetrating, but Nash catches my attention by jumping up and hovering his big head over my phone.

"Sup, Buddy? Is that your girlfriend?" I ask. Once acknowledged, he lies back down.

A minute later he jumps up again and hovers once more.

"Dude, a text message notification comes twice, relax," I explain, while distracted and admiring the veins bulging out of my spent arms.

I wrap up the rest of my workout free of interruptions except for Nash's occasional heavy sighs. I'm not sure why he's so sulky, maybe he's not a fan of my music, but I need to listen to aggressive stuff while I lift weights, it's cathartic for me.

When I finish, my muscles are ripped and full of blood, I've pushed them hard tonight. I take off one sweaty, fingerless glove and toss it at Nash. He jumps up then lowers his chest to the ground, so his tail is wagging furiously in the air. I throw my other glove at him, then peel off and toss my drenched shirt in the general direction of the washer and dryer.

When I finally look at my phone to read the text message, I'm confused. **945 Cedar Avenue** is all it says. Why would someone text me my own address? For his part, Nash barks a deep, resounding bark and then runs up the stairs. My confusion clears a little when I notice the text from Devin has more numbers in the message thread than just mine and his.

Nash is still barking at the front door when I realize what is happening. Shit! I take a whiff of my underarms and confirm I'm a stinky, sweaty, disgusting mess. Well, this ought to do it, I think to myself as I take the stairs two at a time.

I open the door and am not surprised to see Avery standing there. I am highly self-conscious of how I must look and smell, and would rather shut the door in her face than invite her in.

"Hey, what's up?" I ask, for lack of anything better to say.

"Oh, not much. I was just thinking of ordering a pizza and eating it with the biggest manwhore I know. Mind if I come in?" Oh, Jesus. Devin told her everything. When the ground doesn't open up and swallow me whole, I have no choice but to step aside and invite her in with a sweep of my arm.

"I should shower," I deadpan. I am so embarrassed Avery knows about my antics at the club, that I can feel the flush tingle all the way to my scalp.

"Why?" she asks as she smooshes Nash's face between her hands and rocks his big traitorous head back and forth. She's right, I can't wash the nastiness off me with a shower.

"It's just pizza," she says, and then pauses thoughtfully before she continues, "Unless you're thinking of screwing the delivery girl. Then you're right, you should shower." She is smiling. How could she be smiling?

"It's usually an acne riddled guy that brings the pizza."

"Phew, so we dodged that bullet. Are you expecting any door to door solicitors? Or maybe a Hare Krishna or two?"

"Are you done?" I ask, with my head tilted down but my eyes still locked on her green, laughing ones.

She shakes her head *no* while looking at me with a huge shit-eating grin on her face.

"Can we at least order the pizza? I'm starving," I concede.

***

Now that most of the pizza is gone and we have both had a couple of beers, I brace myself and ask, "What exactly did Devin tell you about me?" The fact that she hasn't run screaming from me yet is a little worrisome, but I might as well get everything out on the table.

"He said that you are struggling with something and that you look for distractions between girl's legs. Does that sound right?"

Thank God he didn't go any further with what I'm struggling with or any torrid details. At least I hope he didn't. "I would say that's accurate," I answer.

"What makes you think I want to date or sleep with you anyway?" she asks.

"I don't know, experience maybe," *Fuck*, I sound so pompous I want to punch myself in the face.

"Don't get me wrong, answering the door all sweaty and bare-chested like that might have influenced me a little, but I can't say for sure yet." She sits back on the couch and casually runs her fingers through her hair. She is somehow relaxed. I don't get it.

"Devin the loudmouth told me you are running from something. Is that true?" Ahhhhhh, it feels so good to shift the focus to her.

"He told you that? Really?" Now she feels the treachery bestowed by Devin's squawking mouth. "He made it sound so scandalous," she says with a dramatic, fake shiver.

"You got Mafia after you?" I ask with a genuine smile.

113

"No." She is quiet for a bit, reflective, maybe deciding on how much she is going to tell me. "I left my fiancé. Think that's what he was talking about?" she asks with a dismissive shrug.

My eyes widen before I can control the reaction. Fiancé? Alarm bells are sounding in my head, *Red alert! Red alert!*

"He wasn't good for me, and he disagreed with my appraisal of the situation, so it was better for me to leave." Now she's the one to raise her eyebrows before she takes another sip of beer.

"I'm sorry, that must have been really hard for you." I mean it too, even though I sound like a sapless evergreen.

"Not as hard as you would think. You know how once you're away from a situation, you can finally see it clearly? See it for what it was?"

"Yeah, I do. You said he disagreed with you though, where does that stand right now?"

"It depends on the day, sometimes he's distraught, sometimes filled with rage. It depends on how much he's been drinking."

"Are you in any danger?" I ask, surprised at the realization that my instinct is to protect her.

"Not if he's smart."

"We haven't assessed that yet. But why did you say, *if he's smart?*"

"I have a restraining order against him, that's all." I can tell she doesn't want to elaborate any further, but I still need a few pieces of her elusive puzzle.

"Avery, is this guy coming after you?"

"No. He's too much of a drunk to coordinate all the necessary steps to get here." Her face has lost the teasing glow it always seems to have around me.

I'm silent. I have no fucking idea what to say to that.

"I can see a bruise already forming."

Based on our conversation, it sounds like she is talking about a bruise he gave her, so my mouth drops open, but nothing rolls out.

"Your neck...my kill-shot," she prompts.

Absentmindedly my hand goes to my neck, covering the spot she thwacked with a paintball. I know she's trying to change the subject, and part of me wants her to, but the other part acknowledges how important this conversation is.

Before I can rally my thoughts into a response, she asks, "How long do you think you'll be whoring around before it's out of your system?"

Her question refocuses me immediately. "I don't know, but there's the whole drying out process to think about too," I answer as honestly as I can.

"Does the drying out process involve you waiting for STD results? Or is it more of a figurative term?"

"Figurative. I think it's mostly symbolic of being ready to act like a grown-up again, putting some space between all the meaningless sex and becoming a man of integrity again."

"Ok, so as long as we don't have sex during this 'drying out' phase, you're good with hanging out?" She uses air quotes to drive home her point.

I laugh and realize that yes, I am good with hanging out. It's nice because now that the curtain has been drawn back, I'm not really hiding from anyone anymore.

"That's a relief because I didn't want to have sex with you anyway."

I snort while sipping my beer and the fizz makes my eyes water. "Good, I'm glad that's all cleared up." Then I ask her, "Have you ever been to the driving range?"

"Golf?" she asks, requiring some clarification.

"That or Nascar, we probably should start with golf though."

Chapter Nineteen

Racquetball

It's getting progressively harder and harder not to be intimate with Avery. She is so fucking sexy, and she is good at everything she tries. First, there was paintball, then, after never golfing before, she damn near had a better swing than me at the driving range. Now, it's racquetball. Every time she has a day off, we come here to our echo-y, glassed-in room as soon as I get off of work.

Her shifts at the hospital are twelve hours long, and three times a week, so the other four days we have been battling it out here on the racquetball court. If this is her way of keeping me out of the club, it's working, because her ass in tight workout pants is what the wettest of dreams are made of.

"This only serves to reinforce my feeling that you are a tiny bit competitive. Is that an accurate statement?" I ask as I fire the little blue, rubber ball back at the wall. She is wearing her green bandana like a cap again, and her long braids are coming loose from her exertion.

"What do you expect? I told you, I have three older brothers," she says as she rockets the ball right back. We are both sweating our asses off, and the endorphins are a welcome change from whatever high I was getting from 1462.

Besides staying active, I've been masturbating like a fiend lately, attempting to satiate my carnal desires while still honoring Avery with my abstinence phase. Fuck though, you should see the new calluses I have on my hand.

"Tell me about your brothers, are they all really protective of you," the question comes out with pauses and grunts, the same way she answers back.

"They are very protective of me, thank God I don't live in the same state as them anymore." She's panting, and it's so hot. I bet that is what her face looks like after getting fucked.

"Arghhh! That game's yours, dang it," she says, losing the point, then wiping her forehead with her arm. "Let's get some water, and I'll tell you all about my brothers, the fearsome poets."

We sit with our sweaty backs to the glass wall behind us and both crack open our water bottles.

"Your brothers are poets?" I ask. What are the chances of that? One maybe, but all three?

"We are all named after poets. My mom was a professor, she taught literature," she answers, as if that would explain everything.

"And which poet were you named after? I'm not familiar with an *Avery*, I mean, Silvia for sure, maybe Emily or Margaret, but Avery?" I'm teasing, and she knows it.

"Actually, my name is Dylan Avery Marshall. After Dylan Thomas. Oh, also, I was supposed to be a boy, thus Dylan Thomas as my namesake."

"Dylan Avery is really beautiful. Why don't you go by Dylan?"

"Because I hated it as a kid. It was a scarlet letter, and I burned with indignation at being named after a male poet."

I tip my head against the glass and laugh at her venom. "Yeah you did." Then I drop my head while still giggling, "But don't you mean you, *raged, raged against the dying of the light?*"

"Oh, a comedian are you? Well, you should know I have that particular poem burned on the inside of my eyelids."

"What about your brothers?"

"How well do you know your poetry?"

"I mean, I don't want to brag or anything, but I aced poetry 101 in college," I say, rather confidently. I did ace poetry, but I'm not going to lie, a big part of it was the smoking hot assistant professor. She had extended office hours for students like me. Ones who wanted to study poetry while toying with their professor's nipples under her shirt.

"Let's see then, I'll give you a quote, and you try to guess my brother's names." She cracks her knuckles like this is the point she will blow me out of the water.

"I can resist everything except tempt—"

"Oscar Wilde," I spit out before she can even finish the quote. Then I huff on my fingernails and rub them on my shirt, like an overconfident trivia player. "Your brother's name is Oscar Wilde?" I ask.

"Oscar David actually. That's one point for you, but this gets harder because everyone's familiar with that quote."

"Don't worry, I got this," I'm still way too confident in my poetry recollection after all these years, but getting Oscar Wilde correct gives me a surge of confidence.

"'Genius is the capacity to see ten things where the ordinary man sees one.' Hmm? How about that one?" she asks, confident she has stumped me. Shit, it's familiar…but who said it? I try to drag it from the depths of my brain, but can't quite get it.

"Give me another one."

"Either move or be mov—"

"Ezra Pound!" I shout, before jumping up and celebrating my two for two.

"Yes, Ezra Michael. I'm impressed, Salinger."

"Give me the last one, but first, what do I get if I guess all three?" I crack a smile while I look her up and down like a thirsty pedophile. I'm joking of course, because I'm still not going to sleep with her for a while, maybe even weeks.

"If you get all three, you get a certificate of course. One that says, *I talk a big game, but I'm really committed to my penis cleanse*," she says with a playful glare, her olive green eyes squinting while shooting daggers.

119

"I'll take it. It will remind me of my remarkable poetry recall. And the fact that you want to climb up one side of me, and down the other. Too bad I have to swat you away like a pesky little fly."

"Very funny, are you ready for the last one?"

"Hit me."

"'What happens to a dream deferred? Does it dry up like a raisin in the sun? Or does it explode?'" she finishes, while looking pretty satisfied with herself.

"I'm pretty sure you just made that up," I say.

She laughs, "What about your remarkable poetry recall?" She makes a sad face and pretends to rub her eyes with balled fists.

"Give me another one," I say, nodding and jogging in place.

"'Hold fast to dreams, for if dreams die, life is a broken-winged bird that cannot fly.'"

Shit! "Another," I say with a curt nod.

"You're not going to get it, those were two of his most famous quotes."

"I'll get it."

Sigh, "I have discovered in life that there are ways of getting almost anywhere you want to go."

"Sonofa—" Then I figure I have nothing to lose, so I punt, "Tennyson?"

"Nope."

"I mean, Keats?"

"You're reaching. Do you give up?"

"Robert Frost?"

She folds her arms across her chest and looks at me like a disappointed parent looks at a kid who just stepped in shit.

"Walt Whitman!?"

"No."

"Damn, the only other poet I can think of right now is Poe, and those quotes are too chipper for him."

"Langston Hughes," she says on an exhale.

"It was on the tip of my tongue."

"Don't talk to me about your newly virginal tongue," she says with mock disapproval, then she jumps up and high fives me on the way to her racquet. "Ready for another game?"

She has accepted that I want what she lovingly refers to as a *penis cleanse*, but she doesn't realize that it's not for me. It's for her. I don't want her to feel like she's in the same category as the women I've been fucking for the last few months, and I don't know how to set her apart without putting distance between the two in the form of a *penis cleanse*. It's also important to demonstrate that I don't need the club, and I'm not some sort of sexual deviant either.

You hear talk about muscle memory, well I want to free my penis of all memories from 1462 and the empty mechanics of club fucking. I want to start from scratch—with a clean slate if you will. Not to mention, it's really fun making her squirm, and it's also nice to get to know her without the shroud of sexual haze all around us. Speaking of sexual haze, I've mentioned my new calluses, right?

***

I fall into bed alone again, and this time when Nash hops up, I make him get down. I need to break him of the habit of sleeping with me, and he is none too happy about it. When I start to tug my dick, I'm distracted because he is staring right at me, and his big head is level with my mattress.

"Nash," I say with an authority that he tries his best to ignore. "Go get in your bed."

Sad eyes. Puppy dog eyes in fact.

"Scram, Dude. Go get in your bed," more authority this time. He turns and walks out of my room, but he looks back to see if I've changed my mind no less than three times.

I lie back and picture Avery's big green eyes looking up at me with my dick in her mouth. Those full, pouty lips, her hair falling over her shoulders, and the sloppy sucking sounds her mouth is making. For some reason I always picture her as a slobbery head giver, slurping at my cock, worshiping it as she devours me.

After I spurt all over my abdomen with thick ribbons of warm cum, I leave it there cooling because I'm too lazy to get up. Lately, it doesn't take me long to blow, I think it has to do with the fact that I'm picturing someone who is actually attainable. My former masturbatory material was Jessie, and she was always out of reach, which probably added to her allure. It's probably a good sign my cock is elsewhere when I jerk off, and it certainly makes work a lot easier. Well, that and the fact that Jessie can't keep her head out of the trash can.

I reach for a tissue, sop up the mess, and toss the wet Kleenex in the direction of the master bathroom. I'll pick it up in the morning. As I start to doze off, I reflect on how much fun it is to play hard-to-get with Avery. It's building the sexual tension, and it gives me a sense of control that I haven't felt in *years*. Being hot for Jessie for so long left me feeling like a passenger along for the ride. This thing with Avery feels very powerful, to the point that I might abuse it.

Huh, I would have said I'm not the kind of guy that plays games. Well, what do you know?

Chapter Twenty

Happy Hour

Jessie is in my office looking like a drowned rat and sucking on oyster crackers—her new technique for staving off the hurls—when we both receive a text at the same time. I pull my phone out of my pocket, but she says, "I can't," and leaves it at that. Whether she means she can't deal with retrieving her phone from her lap, or can't deal with whatever task follows the text, I don't know.

"It's from Devin," I announce. "Holy shit! It's Avery's birthday today! How could she not have mentioned that?"

"No one wants a parade on their birthday, Salinger. Not since we were 8 years old anyway. What does Devin propose we do about it?"

"Drinks after work."

"Ok, let's go," she says as she stands up.

"Go where? It's 10:30 in the morning, it's a little early to get a jump on happy hour."

"Don't you want to get her something?" she asks.

"I thought you said, 'no parade.'"

"Yeah, but you need to get her a little something, because Devin and Corey will do some sort of gag gift if I know them at all, and you don't want to be the guy she's seeing who shows up empty-handed. Come on," she says with an exhausted sweep of her arm.

I glance at the string of emails on my computer screen, some of them even marked as urgent, then let out a breath, "All right, let's go."

***

Devin, Corey, Jessie, and I all get to the bar before Avery, which is good because she will be surprised to see us. Not in a surprise party kind of way, but in an Awwwwww kind of way. The guys and I order beers while Jessie nurses a hot chamomile tea.

Silas breezes in, kisses Jessie on the cheek, says hi to the rest of us, and barely sits his ass down before Avery walks in. She's wearing tall boots that lace up the front—that one day I will see her wear with nothing else, tight jeans, a trendy leather jacket, and a smile that could light up the catacombs in Paris. I have the same huge smile on my face but consciously tone it down in order to not look so awestruck.

"I'm so happy you guys are all here!" she says, genuinely excited we all came together for her birthday. What does Jessie know? Every girl wants a little bit of a parade on her birthday. The past few years Jessie and I have kept it pretty simple for birthdays. A couple years ago, she made me a cake and lit the candles right before she walked it into my office. Since then, there has always at least been a cupcake with a candle that we do for each other.

"I think the last one of your birthday parties I attended had a Slip n Slide," Devin laughs.

"I remember that party!" Jessie joins in on the laughter.

I help Avery slide out of her jacket and then lean into her ear from behind, "Happy Birthday, Dylan Avery."

She turns and winks at me. The unspoken sentiment makes me want to drag her into the women's bathroom and fuck her in one of the stalls. There is something to be said for delaying sexual gratification, but damn it's hard.

***

After dinner and a few drinks, right when I'm trying to decide if the penis cleanse has been long enough for a birthday fuck, Devin breaks into my thoughts.

"Ok, we got you a little something special just to remind you how much we all love you," Devin says with a disconcerting glint in his eye.

"Oh, here we go," Jessie says, "I would be worried if I were you. The sweeter his introduction to your gift, the less you are going to want to open it in public."

With a dubious look on her face, Avery reaches into the gift bag and pulls out a deck of cards, but they are not just any cards, they are *dirty talk* cards. She laughs and flips the deck over to read the example on the back.

"I want to lick down your treasure line until I can't go any lower," she blushes a little, and I can see how my penis cleanse is getting under her skin. *Perfect.*

"I'll go ahead and save these for Christmas dinner with my family." She tucks them into her purse.

"There's more, if you can believe it," Corey says through a smile.

She reaches back into the gift bag and pulls out a box of dice. Obviously not run of the mill dice either. These ones have one dice with body parts on the sides, one with an action verb, and one with an adverb. So you might roll, lick, elbow, and gently. Avery's cheeks heat up even more, which makes my balls tighten and my dick chub a little.

"Thank you, Devin and Corey, you guys are so kind to want to help me through a dry spell," she says, as she slowly shakes her head back and forth.

I've gotten used to the idea that everyone at this table knows about my frequent sojourns to 1462, and that I'm holding out on Avery in hopes of, what? Redeeming myself? Cleansing myself? I don't know. This group is so interconnected it seems like nothing is off limits. It's like a really random, patchwork family. I don't even hate Silas anymore, turns out he's a good guy, and he completely adores Jessie—a fact that used to roll my stomach and suffuse me with jealousy.

"Ours is not quite so dramatic. Or presumptuous," Jessie says as she cuts her eyes at Devin. Avery opens the envelope and sees the gift certificate Jessie bought this morning when she was with me.

"Oooooo, a mani/pedi. Thanks, Jessie and Silas!" Avery says, right before she starts to get uncomfortable thinking about how awkward I must be feeling, all empty-handed.

"Who wants to order a brownie sundae?" she asks, quickly moving past the awkwardness.

"Oh wait," Jessie says, as she fumbles in her purse and pulls out a wrapped gift. "Salinger asked me to hold onto this." She passes the gift to me.

I hand it to Avery and say, "I'm a sexual holdout, not an asshole." To which the whole table erupts with good-natured laughter.

She smiles so sweetly at me that my glance toward the restrooms is automatic. The hard-on I'm getting under the table transports me back to middle school, which was full of badly timed boners. Yeah, I've decided birthday sex is in order, for sure.

She unwraps the book and quickly covers her face with her hand. It's a book of Dylan Thomas' work.

"A book of poetry, how eloquent Salinger!" Devin snorts after nearly spitting out his sip of beer.

"I think it's fantastic," Corey tries to recover Devin's snark.

"Oh wait, what's this?" Avery asks as she slides the cabin rental printout from between the pages. "You're taking me to the mountains?" she asks as she lights up.

"Bowww Chicka Woww Woww!" Devin, of course.

"Yeah, but don't worry, the cabin has two bedrooms," I say with a wink that has the same impact on her, that her wink had on me. I can't even remember something so small having such an effect, but the sexual tension between us is crackling like static.

After the waitress clears all of our plates and empty bottles, she wipes the table with a wet rag and sets the bill down between Silas and me. Before she even turns her back to walk away, Jessie starts to gag.

We all look over at her hoping she doesn't toss her cookies in the middle of the bar.

"Oh, God!" she muffles between her fingers, "That rag was sour, can't you smell it?"

"Poor Jessie, she has a dog nose with this pregnancy, I better get her home," Silas says. As they get up and start to collect their things I take the bill and slide my card in. If anyone is going to pick up my girl's birthday happy hour, it's going to be me. And yes, I've decided with certainty that birthday sex is in order. I don't think I can hold out any longer anyway. My body has a visceral reaction to her very presence. I feel like a shark circling a wounded seal, with the tendrils of its blood in the water, dilating my pupils and filling me with an insatiable bloodlust.

"I need to get going too, I have to work tomorrow," Avery says, making my dick slacken with raw disappointment.

Damn.

Chapter Twenty One

Nash

I've taken the day off today because it's D-Day for Nash. It's high time I get him fixed, and the fact he is so excited to go for a ride in the car makes me feel horrendous for what I'm about to put him through. He is so trusting of me, I feel it's only fair to warn him what's in store.

"Listen, Big Guy, you know those coconuts hanging down between your hind legs? Well, you won't be tripping over them anymore. Now, I don't want you to worry too much because chicks dig scars, and you've got those blue eyes, so you'll still turn heads." What I should say, is that balls are overrated, but I spare him my abject grievances.

***

When the vet tech takes him back, I'm a little surprised by the lump in my throat. He's my dog... having a routine procedure, not my kid headed into some complicated life or death surgery. I want to call Avery, but she is working a twelve-hour shift today. The fact that she jumps in a flight-for-life helicopter and swoops in to the rescue is crazy sexy to me. Each time she springs into action, it's only the pilot, a paramedic, and her—the flight nurse. I've seen firsthand how quick and capable someone needs to be in the interest of saving a person's life— active combat will familiarize you with such things.

I wonder how much she knows about my deployments or my injury. The whole group seems to know everything about everyone, including the possibility of Silas being sued over an overdose that happened at the club, and the fact that Corey hums while giving head. These details may seem erroneous or, let's be honest, overshares, but they all add up to a weirdly comforting little niche for me. It's like I have Jessie for work headaches, Silas for club understanding, Corey for military empathy, Devin for comic relief, and Avery…for what? Maybe everything. I can't turn around in this group without being accepted and understood, and I haven't felt those emotions with any degree of continuity in a long time.

My phone vibrates in my pocket, I hope it's Avery. She is able to call or text periodically throughout the day, but I never bug her first, I need to know she isn't intubating someone or otherwise providing critical care before I light up her phone.

It's Jessie, she texts: *How is the big lug doing*?

I text back: *I can only imagine.*

Jessie: *Will you be back here tomorrow*? she asks, probably worried about the stack-up at work.

Me: *I'm keeping it open. I want to see how he is doing before I leave him at home by himself.*

Jessie: *Sounds like you want an extra long weekend to me.*

Me: *You might be right. Can you keep your head out of the trash can while I'm gone*?

Jessie: *That remains to be seen.*

***

Nash is groggy and sluggish when they bring him out. When he spares me a glance then looks quickly away, I feel like a cruel bastard. A responsible pet owner, but still a cruel bastard. He's walking toward me really slow and hanging his head as if even he knows he's been emasculated. Or, his demeanor could be attributed to the giant cone around his head.

"He did great," the vet tech announces as she takes a seat in the chair perpendicular to mine, then uncomfortably runs her hands up and down the thighs of her scrub pants. She seems nervous to make eye contact with me, so the interaction is already awkward. I wonder if she's nervous to talk about balls with me?

"I'm glad he did well...it's weird though, for some reason, I feel like having a martini," I say, referencing the cone in a stupid attempt to loosen her up.

She laughs a little too hard at my lame joke, and then says, "We call it the Cone of Shame."

Now that she finds me more approachable, if not a little bizarre, I ask, "How long does he need to wear it?"

"Until the incision completely heals, about 5-7 days," she looks at Nash while she answers, but he doesn't give two shits about what she is saying.

While she's going over the rest of the post-operative care instructions, I know I should be paying attention, but my phone is vibrating in my pocket. The simple fact I usually get texts instead of calls makes me certain it's Avery. I'm inwardly struggling, should I be rude and answer the phone, or wait until she gets another chance to call me?

Turns out the decision is made for me, in the form of a motionless phone. Ironically, seconds after my phone stills, the tech looks me shyly in the eyes and asks if I have any questions. I do not, especially because she already handed me the aftercare printout with all the same information.

"Nope, are we good to go now?"

She hands me the end of Nash's leash and smiles, "Yep, you're all set, please call us if you have any questions, Mr. Davis." Then she stands and gives Nash a cursory tap on his back.

"Will do. Thanks for the castration." I can't resist this last little bit of humor because of the reaction I know it will draw. Just as I suspect, she blushes from her scalp to her non-slip clogs.

Chapter Twenty Two

Check-In

Now that I've decided to end the cleanse, I can't get Avery over here fast enough. She may have dashed my hopes of birthday sex by needing to get home, but now, *it's on.* I know she's off today after a couple long days at work. She thinks I'm back at the office now, so I've asked her to stop by and check on Nash this afternoon.

Instead of going back to work, I spend the day cleaning and washing my sheets in preparation of having sex with her for the first time, after *a lot* of buildup.

After the house is cleaner than it's ever been, I head to the basement for a workout. After that, I'll have just enough time for a shower. Nash has been a bum and mostly slept for the last day and a half, but otherwise, he's no worse for the wear. In fact, I have factored him in to my devious plan.

***

I hear Avery when she lets herself in, and I know Nash has gone straight to the door to greet her, because I hear her laugh and say, "What have you got there, Nash?"

Earlier today, I fashioned a green olive out of some Icynene spray-foam from the garage, and a little paint. Then I attached it to Nash's collar so he would look like a proper martini. He hates having the added burden inside his detestable cone, and he keeps trying to dump it out, which is just as hilarious as it sounds.

On the improvised olive, is a note for Avery to open the fridge. When she goes to the fridge, with Nash, no doubt trailing right behind her, she finds a pink lily and another note.

By the time she finishes the scavenger hunt, which ends in my bedroom, she has amassed a bouquet of pink lilies and a big smile on her face that doesn't match the red and swollen eyes, leftover from crying.

"Avery, what's wrong?" I jump up from the foot of the bed and go straight over to her. As soon as she is wrapped in my arms, she starts crying in earnest.

"Oh, wow. This is not the reaction I was expecting. Would you have preferred white lilies?" I say, trying to elicit a laugh out of her and make light of the whole thing. She tries to speak while nestled against my chest but only cries harder.

"Avery, is it your ex-fiancé? Has he done something to you?" This is the only thing I can think of because there is still so much more to *that* story than I know about. This ex of hers is a wildcard for me until she opens up more about him.

She shakes her head *no* and tries to take some deep breaths to calm down. I smooth her hair with my hand and kiss her head. Something terrible has happened, and I'm helpless to do anything until she can talk to me. I have a million different scenarios running through my mind, but much like trying to catch a fly with your bare hand, the reason for her distress eludes me.

After several long minutes—or ten, she sucks in a breath, sharply, like she wasn't expecting it and then pulls her face away from my chest.

"Tell me. What I can do?" I say, and it sounds ridiculous, but I'm a problem solver by nature. The problem is that I don't decode cryptic evidence and sew together clues very well. I'm more black and white.

"It's always... the... kids," she sniffles.

"Who's kids? Is someone hurt?" I'm grasping at even flimsy hints. Her beautiful face is so distraught, and when ringed in red, her eyes are electric green.

"That I…take care of," she closes her eyes and slowly shakes her head back and forth, as if trying to erase it from her memory.

I ease her down to sit on the end of the bed with me, and I kiss her forehead because now I know what's wrong, but I don't have a damn thing to say. I tuck her against my side and cradle her face with my palm.

"Avery, I'm so sorry," It's pathetic, I know this, but words escape me.

"He asked me if he was going to die…" she brings her hand up to cover her face as a new wave of unshed tears floods her eyes, "And I told him, no."

"Oh my God! Avery, I'm so sorry." I can feel it creeping in under my flesh. The familiar, prickling anxiety. It's as recognizable as the glasses on my face, and it makes me feel like I need to shed my skin. For me, the anxiety is that feeling of knowing…*knowing* there is nothing you can do to bring them back no matter how bad you want to. This is about more than Avery's patient for me right now, there are feelings bubbling to the surface that I haven't acknowledged in a very long time, and it nearly paralyzes me.

A few minutes crawl by while I try to tamp down my own dark and menacing demons. This is not about me, this is not about me, *this is not about me*. Avery needs my support right now.

"He died in my arms, Salinger."

I try to think of something quick, something that will take the sting off that last statement. "I'm glad he had someone like you to hold him and comfort him in the end." It's all I've got, and it's pretty weak.

"We didn't stop. We kept at it until we were on the critical care unit." She is overcome again, "I was straddling his little body on the pram while they wheeled us in. I never would have stopped CPR, Salinger…some of the Physicians had to pull me off of him."

I feel a tear streak down my cheek. I don't know how she does it. She has a beautiful soul, and is tough as nails, but a child you are trying to save dying in your arms is enough to make anyone break.

"Avery, I want you to think of all the people who are alive today because of you. All the other kids that you brought back."

"It's not enough," she says. Her inflection is flat, and I know exactly how she feels. That was my voice for more than a year after the IED.

"It *is* enough. Humans have limitations for what we can do. I know you wanted to save him, but his injuries were fatal. Honey, that's not on you."

"I keep thinking if I had done something different or if we got there faster—"

"Avery, it was a horrible accident, you could have done things a thousand different ways...and he still would have passed." I think about telling her, *it was his time to go,* but I can't even get that phony, plastic statement out of my mouth. As far as I'm concerned, it's never a kid's time to go. That little boy should have lived to see his great-grandchildren.

"But, what if—"

"His injuries were fatal, and you were able to offer him peace in his last moments. You are a very special person." I pull her tighter into me and wrap my other arm around her. This woman is exactly the kind of person I need in my life. The kind that cares too much. The kind that gives everything of herself and still wants to give more. The kind who's heart is so open that sometimes she has to fall apart just so she can put herself back together stronger and more formidable for next time.

I think I'm already in love with her. We've only been seeing each other for a few weeks, and we haven't even slept together yet, but yes, I already love her.

She pulls back from me, steady and no longer on the brink of tears. "How did you know I needed these?" she asks, as she holds up the bouquet of lilies that she had been holding behind my back.

I grab her face and kiss both of her swollen eyes, and then her mouth. It's better if I keep it to myself that the flowers were supposed to evolve into hot sex, and that I had planned on having her every which way I could. To my screeching disappointment, tonight is definitely not the right night. There will be no sex on these clean sheets tonight.

At this point, we've waited too long to fall sloppily into bed. Maybe our trip to the mountain cabin over New Year's would be a more appropriate setting for our first time together. Too bad that's so fucking far away.

It's only four in the afternoon, so I suggest, "How about we order Chinese food and watch a whole season of something on TV?"

"I would love that," she says, and the smile lights up her sad face.

***

It's getting late. We are about midway through some angsty TV series that I've had a hard time focusing on because of everything going on in my brain. To start with, this whole no sex thing is unchartered territory for me. Normally, if it gets late and I'm with a girl, we just—go to bed together. But if I do ask her to stay, my cock will pitch a tent to rival that of a KOA campground all. night. long. Which leads me to the fact that I wouldn't be able to rub one out, and would probably end up jealous of Nash's situation because of my own taut and aching blue balls.

If I'm really going to analyze the whole thing, which apparently I am, how could I even sleep next to her without it turning into sex? I'd like our first time to be at the cabin, but I'm not a superhero, so I know my dick would find its way into her. All she would have to do is brush against it while we were kissing and that's all it would take.

The other major distraction of my television focus is that I have been as desperate as a naked panhandler to keep my cock down. I'm lying down on my back with one knee bent and resting against the back of the leather couch. Comfortable, loungy, even relaxed if you don't factor in Avery's absentminded cock tease. She is lying on her stomach, kind of hugging my waist and resting the side of her face on my chest.

My dick has been trying for hours to get hard, and I've done everything possible to keep it down. Some guys think about sports stats in this situation but that doesn't work for me, I have to think about sticking jagged urethral rods down my penis hole, or performing oral sex on a diseased homeless person, and other equally disturbing things. At one point, I even considered busting a nut in the bathroom when I was in there to pee. The only reason I didn't is because it felt lecherous, and knowing how perceptive Avery is she would have known it straight away.

When the episode ends, I literally have no idea what is going on in the show. She turns her head and looks at me with her chin on my chest.

"I wasn't expecting that! Were you?"

Oh God, it's plot twist trivia time. I take a swing, "Not at all." Apparently, my vague answer is enough to satisfy her question, but the bigger problem now is that she scoots up my body and plants a kiss on my lips.

"I need to get going, but let's go have fondue tomorrow." She says it like a statement, not a question. I'm so relieved she sidestepped the whole overnight thing that I almost sigh with relief.

"You got it. I'll pick you up at seven," I say. Then I palm her cheek and bring her in for another kiss. Damn it, this is where I unravel. Our kisses so far have been pretty chaste, but this one is not, and she is on top of me. *Fuck*! The whole penis cleanse was a stupid idea, and long after I was ready for it to be over, I still teased her with it. It felt good to be pursued. But fuck it! I can't keep up this charade anymore. I want inside her so bad I can almost taste her pussy.

For the record, she is the one who breaks the kiss. I would have ridden that wave all the way to shore.

"Remember, I'm heading back to Seattle on Sunday for Christmas. Speaking of Christmas, I propose we exchange little token gifts when we go to the mountains. How does that sound?"

My eyes feel gauzy with lust, "Sounds good to me." *You know what else sounds good to me? You sitting on my face right now.*

I walk her to the door, where she reaches inside Nash's cone and grabs his cheeks before planting a firm kiss on his dopey head. When she hesitates at the door, it's all the encouragement I need.

I pull her against me and kiss her soundly, this time I know she can feel me stiffening and I don't even care. My dick is like a homing device, and it's found its way. I want her bad. So bad in fact, my body is humming with the need to fuck her.

"Goodnight, Salinger."

"Goodnight, Avery."

Hello, blue balls.

Chapter Twenty Three

Alone

With Christmas only days away, I spend my morning ordering gifts online and then paying a king's ransom to have the shipping expedited. This year Christmas is going to be pretty anti-climactic for me. My sister always travels for the holidays, so her absence is nothing new. She is a do-gooder, last year she went to Hati to help build houses, and this year she's digging wells in Costa Rica.

I don't relish the idea of her going alone this year, but that douchebag of a live-in broke her heart and took off. I even considered going with her, if that tells you anything about how dull my holidays have become, but my passport was expired, and that was all the excuse I needed not to go.

Anyway, with my mom in Florida now, I won't be spending Christmas with her either. I could have bought a plane ticket, she wanted me to, but honestly, she would have had a line of eligible bachelorettes in and out of the house for the entire duration of my stay. My mom is ready for me to repopulate the earth with her grand-babies, and she's about as subtle as a loose chainsaw.

Jessie, Silas, Ruby, Devin, and Corey are all flying to Jessie's parent's house, where, with her parents and siblings gathered around the Christmas tree, they will reveal Jessie's knocked-up state. That ought to be fun. Mom, Dad, I'm having a baby, and then I'm giving your grandchild to Devin and Corey to raise. That should throw some cold water on the grandparent's Christmas joy. Although, you know, Devin is really a part of their family, so maybe it will shake out just the same for them.

Every year without fail, a couple of my college buddies invite me to attend their respective holiday parties. The beauty of Christmas time is that there are a ton of holiday parties, which make for convenient excuses to have other plans. It's a knee jerk reaction for me at this point. Being the token single guy at shit like that makes you a prime target for everyone and their brother to try and set you up with someone they know who happens to have a vagina and a heartbeat.

Fuck no. I mean, I'm sorry, I already have plans that night, that's the *exact* same night of my company holiday party. Some years my company holiday party even extends to multiple weekends.

Last night when Avery asked why I didn't have a Christmas tree up, I didn't know what to say. I mean, do single guys with no kids decorate for the holidays? I can see it now, my lonely childhood Christmas stocking hanging from the roughhewn mantle that I built myself two years ago. No thank you.

I decide to go for a hike to burn the rest of the day, and Nash is absolutely beside himself with glee until he realizes he will not be joining me.

"Sorry, Bud, you heard the vet. No strenuous activity for two weeks." I raise my hands and shrug, but I don't actually feel bad because I'm taking the steep side of the incline up to the peak, and he's not stealthy enough for blazing a trail up that arduous of a climb. He is all knees and legs on a regular day, so this hike needs to be a solo mission for me.

He can't believe his bad luck, so he walks over to deposit his sad, cone-headed self on his dog bed to pout. I think about seeing if Avery wants to go, but in the end, I figure I will see her in a few hours anyway.

I give Nash a marrow bone on my way out, which should keep him busy because he'll have to figure out a way to chew it with a foghorn around his neck. I usually make him take bones outside, but I feel kind of bad leaving him behind, especially when he can smell the hike on me.

***

The maddening thing about fondue is that it takes almost three hours just to roll through the required elements of cheese, broth, and chocolate. It's certainly not the kind of place you want to go if you don't have a connection with someone. Due to our frenetic sexual energy and intense connection, I'm happy to be here with Avery for all three hours of melted food.

For the past month, we have seen a lot of each other, but it's usually somewhere neutral and doing something active and sweaty. This is the reason I'm all but stupefied by how hot she is. Don't get me wrong, she's fucking beautiful in a hat and braids or ponytail, without wearing much makeup but tonight...holy shit. She has glittery orange makeup around her eyes that makes them look so green they seem liquid and bottomless, and her lashes—all I can think about is her looking up at me with those dark lashes while my cock is in her mouth. Gah! She is fucking mesmerizing, and she definitely came with the big guns tonight. She's not fucking around anymore, not at all.

"Don't you think?"

"Hmmm, what?" I snap to attention.

"I said, we should go get you a Christmas tree and decorate it tonight," she repeats with a grin as she winds cheese around the hunk of green apple on the tip of her fondue fork.

"Yeah, we could do that," I say, while my brain scrambles for where I would even find my holiday decorations. I haven't so much as thought about looking for that bin since my divorce. I'm not even sure I am still in possession of it.

She roots around in her purse for a minute, then pulls out a silver snowflake Christmas ornament, and then hands it over to me. "We can put this on it. Our first ornament together."

I smile, but what I really want to do is slide my arm behind her waist and pull her around the corner of our U-shaped booth onto my lap. She is sitting at a ninety-degree angle to me, but fairly close, I could do it.

The restaurant is designed so each table is secluded from the others, but the damn server is so attentive. If he's not mixing our fondue while explaining each solitary ingredient, he is bringing more cubes of bread, or topping off our ice water, or offering another beer for me or glass of wine for her.

"I like that idea. It may be a lonely ornament until next year though." Neither of us misses the mention of being together next year. She did the same thing though, our *first* ornament together.

Christ, she's hot. Damn fondue for its three-hour commitment, and damn my ridiculous penis cleanse. We should already have been fucking for weeks now. This isn't natural, I should already have her body memorized and know her sexual likes and dislikes.

"Oh look," Avery says as she pulls another item out of her purse, "I forgot all about this, let's open it." She has a mischievous glint in her eyes that I don't entirely trust. Knowing she's holding the gift from Devin and that it's paired with her playful smirk, I start to worry that she's going to punish me a little for making *her* wait.

"Is it the cards or the dice?" I ask, praying it's the dice. If it's the dice, we can't very well play here.

"The dirty talk cards!" she says with a phony mask of innocence all over her face.

Shit.

"I don't know how we're supposed to play, especially here, but you take half, and I'll keep half. We can read them one at a time to each other. Don't cherry-pick through them either, you have to read the card on top of your stack." Then she rubs her hands together like an evil genius, and I know I've already lost the game. And it *is* a game at this point. She wants to torture me because now she knows I'm weak. She knows I would have fucked her up against my front door last night if she hadn't broken off our kiss. *Ok penis, let's try to keep our game face on.*

"You first," she says.

I take the top card, read it to myself, and then look her in the eyes, thankful it's a mild one. I hope they are all bush league like this card.

"I want to nuzzle your neck," I say.

She seems disappointed by the novice level of the cards. Not me, it's hard enough to keep my pecker down when I'm around her without introducing dirty, sex talk.

She silently reads her top card, and then looks up at me, "I want to tickle your back with my penis slash nipples." Then she scrunches up her nose, "They are all going to be for either sex, let's just apply the correct one when we read it."

"Got it," I say, then take a deep breath, "I want to kiss and drag my tongue all over the sway of your lower back." Still tame, so far so good.

"Salinger, I want to suck one of your balls into my mou—"

"How are we doing here?!" fuck nut asks, as he charges the table and starts clearing the cheese course and it's requisite dippers, "Are you ready for the broth fondue now, or would you like to give it a few minutes?"

"How about a few more minutes?"

"Now is good," we answer at the same time. Shit, I want this three-course dinner transaction over as soon as possible so I can get Avery in my bed.

He claps his hands in a goofy way, and then parks them on his hips, "Now...which one is it, you two?" His teeth are huge, I don't think I've ever seen such big teeth.

"Give us five minutes please," Avery says.

Once our service clown leaves, she turns her devious eyes on me, "Your turn."

Do people get fondue to go? I wonder to myself. Then, I read the card. *Fuck! Fuck! Fuck!* I take a deep breath in preparation of repeating this doozy of a card.

"Avery, I want to tickle my fingers against your wet panties, and then slide my hand inside them." Gulp. Check please.

145

"Oooooo, is that right?" She is playing with me. This feels like payback. "Well, Salinger... I want to taste the head of your cock while I drag my tongue all over it."

"I can't do this," I say, laughing and throwing up my hands. "I'm out."

"Come on, just a few more," she says as she slides a little closer. She smells like clean, scented lotion and it heats up the back of my neck.

I hesitantly reach for the top card, then pause for effect, "I want to lick your sopping wet pussy until you come all over my face," I look her right in the eyes and speak quietly, so she has to lean in a little closer, a fly about to get tangled in my sticky web.

She looks up at me with something different in her eyes, she's not teasing for once. She slides closer, right next to me and then leans in to my ear, whispering, "Salinger, I want to feel your huge cock sliding in and out of my tight pussy until the clenching of my orgasm milks every bit of cum from your body... And then, I want to do it all over again." Her hand is stroking my granite penis, and it didn't escape my notice, by the way, that she never did grab a card, she freestyled that one like a fucking pro. I lower my chin and kiss her mouth, while she eases my zipper down.

There is so much heat in our kiss after having to stifle our desire for so long, that I don't give two shits when our toothy waiter waltzes back in, freezes for a few seconds and then backs himself out of the tiny room. He couldn't possibly see my hard, naked cock in her hand under the table, but he could see the way I held her next to me and how I was kissing her. My palm is holding her jaw, with my fingers feathered into her hair and there is heat, so much fucking heat for only being one-third of the way through dinner.

I drop my hand to her thigh then slide my fingers under her dress, tickling my way up. I groan when I feel her stockings give way to bare skin and *garters*. Oh, fuck...this is my dream woman.

"Open for me," I breathe into our kiss, as my palm drifts up the inside of her smooth thigh. I'm turned in the booth, so the way my arm is positioned up the inside of her thigh, with my exploring fingers, there can be no question as to what's happening if the waiter comes back now.

Her strokes up and down my cock are slow, deliberate and because she pays particular attention to the ridge of my head, it makes me want to blow my load right here.

My fingers find her satin panties and tug them away from her warm body just enough to slide my fingers under them right where her legs come together. My knuckles brush against her bare pussy, she's hot and slick, and I'm losing all desire to remain socially acceptable. An indecent exposure or public lewdness charge is not even enough right now to slow me down. I want my mouth on her right now, separating her crease with my tongue—more than all the fondue in the world.

I start with simply drifting my knuckles over her naked pussy lips, just a tickle, only a hint of contact. It's driving her crazy because she widens her legs even more for my touch. She's aching for me. I have no intention of hurrying, and besides, she's the one who lit this fuse. I withdraw my hand to dip my fingers into the glass of ice water while cradling the back of her head with my other hand to deepen our kiss.

This time when I move her panties over and find her clit with my chilled thumb, she moans loudly into my mouth, unable to stifle the sound before it's already out. The unexpected contrast of my cold thumb against such naked heat has her sucking on my bottom lip and biting down in an effort to still her panting.

I'm intent on getting her off before I blow, so along with the rhythmic pressure of my thumb, I press two fingers inside her pussy. The way her body accepts me, swallowing my fingers into the silkiness of her body, makes me think of nothing except pressing my cock deep into the same dewy slit. I glide my fingers in and out, curling them against the rougher texture of her g-spot.

She rolls her head back and whispers to the ceiling, "I'm going to come, Salinger." It's almost polite and refined the way she says it, but it's so hot to see her like this and to hear her restrained announcement. I feel my own orgasm tighten, just before the breach.

"Ave, grab the napkin," I can barely choke it out in time for her to drop the napkin over her other hand and my spouting cock. I pull her face against mine with my free hand behind her neck, and we shiver against our climaxes with our mouths pressed together.

Everything is perfectly still for a minute, and I realize my fingers are still buried in the warm clasp of her body. I slide them slowly out, then fiddle with her perfectly slicked lips. I slide my wet fingers over them, between them, and finally, I gently tug on them. I want to learn her body. I want to know every nuance of it because I plan on being inside her every chance I get.

She may be doing the same thing, learning my body because she is lightly smearing my cum all over and around my half-stiff dick.

I have detached my fingers from her body before our waiter arrives again; first announcing his imminent arrival with a hearty cough, but she still has my cock in her hand.

The whole time he chatters on, adjusting the heat of the fondue pot and hastily preparing the broth, she swipes her thumb back and forth across my head. My penis is covered by the napkin, but her hand is very obviously moving beneath it.

Our waiter is uncomfortable enough to rattle off the instructions about not touching the raw meat to our plate and explaining the different dipping sauces in about three breaths, before making himself scarce. I don't know if he witnessed any part of Avery's fingering, or if he was drowning in all the pheromones in here, but I don't care.

I don't even want to stay for the last two courses if you want to know the truth. All I can think about is laying Avery naked across my bed and spreading her open. I've already been inside of her, but I've never even seen her tits. Just thinking about her hard nipples under this dress makes my cock start to stiffen again.

Then she does something that shocks me entirely. She lets go of my dick and brings two cum coated fingers straight to her lips. She is looking me right in the eyes as she sucks them into her sexy mouth. Now my dick is definitely feeling a new surge of blood, so I take this opportunity to tuck the wiley thing back into my pants where it can at least be contained.

"I've wanted to taste you for a long time," she says as she licks her full lips.

"Avery, the feeling is entirely mutual," I say, just before smiley comes back in with a tray of chicken, steak, shrimp, and lobster.

Chapter Twenty Four

Boom

We get back to her apartment, and before the door even closes behind us, I've lifted her to my hips. She wraps her legs around me, and her short dress falls back against her hips to hang limply behind her. The position has her legs wide open against me, and save for the fabric of her panties and my pants, my dick would already be inside her. It's dark in her apartment, and I've only been here a few times; briefly at that, so I'm fumbling around for a light while carrying her with me, as I stumble into coffee tables and trip over laptop cords.

She is giggling against my mouth, but it doesn't negate the raw carnality of our kissing. The last few weeks have clearly bottled up inside both of us. We are unhinged in our movements and clawing at each other's clothes.

I make it to the kitchen and smack the rocker switch on the wall just before I dump her on the polished concrete countertop. The counter is wide and has barstools on the other side of it, so there is plenty of room to lay her out. The kitchen is bright, owing to the overabundance of recessed cans in the relatively small space, but I have to lay eyes on her body.

She unbuttons a few buttons on my shirt, then gives up and pulls it and my t-shirt over my head. The tops of her bare thighs are visible along with the black garter belt straps that have her looking like a vintage, pin-

151

up model. She is hastily unbuttoning the front of her dress, so I get a glimpse of her black bra against her pale, perfect skin before my eyes are drawn back to the garters.

I reach under her ass, grab her panties from behind and pull them off. The clever girl has worn her panties over the garters, further evidence that this whole sex thing is no accident.

While I'm frantically yanking her panties off each of her black stilettos, she leans back on her hands and casually lifts a leg to contribute to their removal. I get on my knees and drag her hips forward to the edge of the counter. Oh my God! I can smell her arousal and see her bare pussy right in front of my face. The raunchy view is so fucking sexy, but I want much more, so I push her legs even further apart.

She has her head thrown back with her hands bracing herself on the counter behind her. In this position, her tits are pushed forward while the unbuttoned top of her dress falls open. Her tits are showcased in a lacy bra, and her legs are wrenched widely apart.

I stop for a moment, mesmerized while I stare at the obscene perfection of her, I want to commit this exact pose to memory. I don't think I've ever seen something so erotic in my life.

She groans with impatience and brings a hand up to cup her breast. I can't take it anymore, I have to taste her. I use my fingers to spread her lips and expose her rawness to me, then I advance my tongue on her pinkness. I was right, she does taste like a warm, ripe peach.

My tongue is everywhere; I glide it over and over her wet silk, drinking her in and still dying of thirst. I press my tongue in and out of her tight vagina, and I tap it against her clit. Once she has the fingers of one hand tightly gripping my hair, and she's writhing beneath my touch, I focus entirely on her sweet clit. I rub it and flick it, and suck on it until she stiffens and exclaims, "Oh, Salinger! Yes! Just like that!" Her legs start to shake so her next statement comes as no surprise, "Ooooooh, I'm coming, oh, yessss!" and then she explodes around me, almost violently, as I cradle her naked pussy against my face. I love how she orgasms, she's vocal and authentic. I'm going to jerk off to this very moment the whole time she's in Seattle.

She lies back on the counter breathless, as I lessen the pressure of my tongue, but don't stop completely. This is often my favorite part. Her clit is swollen and intensely sensitive, and her silky flesh is almost vibrating against my tongue. She raises one leg to drape a thigh over my shoulder but leaves the other one spread wide. I love her confidence, a lot of women would not just lie back and let someone become so acquainted with their fully illuminated, naked, and spread open vagina.

"Nobody has ever licked my pussy so good," she says on an exhale, making me chuckle as I stand up. The compliment makes the throbbing pain in my knees a little more bearable.

"Come to the couch," I say, as I hoist her up by one arm. If I don't get my dick inside her soon, I'm not going to be able to walk tomorrow.

We walk to the living room, me still clothed from the waist down, and Avery, clothed but with the top of her dress unbuttoned and open down the front. We both drop down on the couch.

"I feel like I should put on music or light candles or something. I mean, this is it right? The big event? The end of the penis cleanse?" she asks, as if it were even up for debate.

"Avery?" I say, and it sounds like a question, or a reproach maybe.

"Yes?" she asks, widening her eyes.

"I'm going to fuck you so hard, you'll need to wear a tight skirt tomorrow just to keep your legs together."

"Sounds promising, but first…" she gets on her knees between my legs and unfastens my pants. My dick has been hard for the majority of the evening and certainly for the last forty-five minutes, she might get a black eye if she isn't careful. Then she continues, "I have some reciprocating to do. I can't wait to suck your cock, Salinger. Your dick has been on my mind for a very long time." Just hearing those words come out of her sweet mouth is filthy, and it's fucking fantastic.

She tugs off my shoes and socks, then eases my pants and boxer briefs down with a little help from me raising my hips, and then tugs them completely off. Then she leans all the way forward against my naked body and starts kissing me.

After a while I say, "This has to go," as I ease her dress off the backs of her shoulders. She stands up and lets it fall off so that it pools around her feet. My mouth hangs partway open as I look at her. She is wearing nothing but heels, thigh highs with a black garter belt—no panties, and a black lace bra.

"You might as well take that off too," I say as my heart starts beating faster. She reaches behind her back and unhooks her bra, never taking her eyes off mine. I'm torn about keeping eye contact or looking at her tits as soon as the bra falls.

She gradually moves the lace away from her chest, then holds it out to me and drops it in my lap. There is no question about breaking eye contact now, as my eyes shoot to her perky tits and hard nipples. I've already fingered her and eaten her out, but this is my first look at her amazing rack. She stands there, knowing my attention is rapt, and revels in it. I've seen her nipples through shirts or workout tops before, but seeing them naked is a new experience, and my cock starts to sway with impatience.

"Do you have a condom?" she asks.

Then I panic a little, picturing the black and gold box of them in my nightstand, "No, do you?"

"What if I don't?" she asks as she starts to toy with her nipples. She is still standing in front of me mostly naked, and now she's putting on a show.

"That's a deal breaker for me," I say, not that I wouldn't crawl to the nearest convenience store if I had to.

"I was hoping you would say that," she says, pretty satisfied with herself.

"Wait, what? Why?" I stammer, not understanding her meaning.

"Because your penis needed a cleanse, that's why. And because you are a man-whore. I wouldn't want to pick something up from the club. But, if it's a deal breaker for you, then you've always worn one. Right?"

"Always, do you have some or not?" I sound really impatient...*because I am.*

"Yeah." Now she's tugging her nipples while still displayed in front of me.

"Aves, I'm about to bend you over this couch."

She gets back on her knees and leans forward again, pressing my erection between her tits. Then she plants a kiss on my chest and slowly works her way down. I've got both of her nipples pinched between my fingers until they pull free, out of my reach. Which is just about the same time she closes her mouth around my cock, and I see stars.

I'm slouched down on the couch, and I'm watching her suck my dick just like I pictured it, with her big green eyes and dark lashes looking up, right at me. Upon further reflection, I'm glad I already got off at the fondue joint, because I wouldn't be able to take much more of this with a full sack.

Her mouth is warm and wet, and the sucking sounds that accompany her enthusiastic blowjob are what wet dreams are made of. She stops sucking and begins to ring my cock head with her tongue. My head wants to fall back, but I can't take my eyes off how she is savoring my cock. After the tongue circling particular bit of ecstasy, she curls the tip of her tongue and drags it back and forth over my frenulum until I'm clenching my teeth and rendered unable to stop her, even for sex. One of my legs is quaking, and I have to look away from her eye contact just to extend the euphoria I'm feeling.

When she closes her mouth on me again, it's only a formality because the orgasm is here.

Some girls like a warning before the surge, so I attempt one, "I'm, gah! Gonna—"

She acknowledges me by humming, "Uh, huh" against my shaft, as if it were the most obvious conclusion in the world, and it is because just now I let it rip. The level of intensity exiting my cock leaves me useless in a jaw clenching, vein popping, agonizing groan, which quickly turns into a laugh from such a thorough release.

She backs off my rod and creeps up my body, dribbling cum as she advances. When she starts to rub her tits in the still-warm ejaculate, I grin like a lunatic because it's the hottest thing I've ever seen done with cum.

She climbs up to straddle my body with my hands on her hips. Then she blows my mind when she sits back and starts to fondle her semen coated nipples.

"What time is your flight in the morning?" I ask, not even able to rip my eyes away from her sticky tits and swollen nipples.

"I have to leave at five a.m," she glances at the clock on the wall, it's just after midnight now.

"Five hours. Good, because I'm not even close to being done with you."

I pull her closer against my body, and her knees disappear between the oversized cushions that make up the back of her couch. Now she is pressed against me, and there is no fabric between us.

I start kissing her mouth as my hands go straight to her tits, but I am highly cognizant of the fact her bare pussy is resting against my stomach. I'm torn about whether I should tend to her clit, or keep playing with her rigid nipples. I decide to stick with her tits, they are now cold from the chilled ejaculate, and I want to play with them all night.

When she leans her whole upper body into mine, I can feel her cold, hard nipples against my chest and it gives me the chills down the backs of my arms. My hands move against her sides so my thumbs can scrape roughly back and forth over her nipples, even though they are pressed tightly against my body.

She is grinding her pelvis against me, and it's getting me riled up again, but I want to slow things down a bit. Moving my hands down to her ass I grip her cheeks, and the thought of that simple action causing her lips to part is enough to stiffen my cock again.

With our mouths in perfect harmony, I lower one hand down between her legs from behind. I find her satiny entrance and flutter my fingers against it, toying with her for a little while. When she starts to moan and arch her back, granting me easier access, I dip in.

Then I press my middle finger fully into her vagina. As I glide it in and out, I can feel her slow down our kisses then stop entirely, leaving her mouth next to mine but still a breath away.

She wrenches her head back which only brings her tits closer to my face. Naturally, I immediately pinch her nipple between my lips. I'm surprised at first by the taste of my cum, but soon all I can think about is her beautiful naked breasts right in front of me. My free hand finds the same nipple to pinch and twist as my mouth moves over to the other cum flavored one.

"Salinger, please," she whines, "Please, I need you to fuck me."

Hearing her say that is like entire choirs of angels singing. I gently bite down on her nipple and pinch the other one a little harder, as I lean back from her panting body, tugging her nipples with me until they pull free.

"Where are the rubbers?" I ask, now I'm the one panting.

"In my purse, awww," she croons while my finger still plunges in and out of her.

"Get one."

She rests her forehead against mine for a few seconds collecting herself, then she climbs off my lap on shaky legs. I'm proud of my penis for rallying, but I'm not at all surprised. In fact, I may have a perma-boner from here on out.

She tears the condom open and then tries to unroll it down my shaft, but her hands are shaking too much. I take it from her and sheath my cock with it.

"Are you ok with this? Are you nervous?" I ask, she seems scared to death, and it's probably because she thinks I've been with a million women.

"No...I'm not nervous. I just want you so bad."

At the risk of sounding like a total pussy, my heart melts with her admission. It's her emotion... her intensity, she's got me. It's all over for me now.

I take her hand and help her straddle my lap again. I put my hand on the back of her neck and urge her closer to me, "And *I* want *you* so bad."

Normally, I would take charge and run the show, but with us on the couch instead of a bed, and not wanting to fuck her on the floor for our first time, she's going to be on top. Plus I haven't had nearly enough of her tits in my face. You may be wondering why we don't go to her bedroom, and the answer is simple—it's too fucking far away, and I need her right now.

She puts her arms around me, holding me tightly as I direct the tip of my cock into her pussy. Then she eases herself down, slowly and completely. I can feel her silky resistance as I bore through her, her vagina clamping around me from every possible angle.

"You feel so good," I whisper, hardly making a sound, then kiss her neck as she eases herself up. There is the feel of suction as my cock withdraws, then that harmonious, exquisite resistance. I hug her tightly to my body, not wanting to miss a second of our union. It's slow and tender as our naked bodies fuse together with sweat.

This is nothing how I thought sex with Avery would go. I thought we'd be clawing at each other, desperate to get inside one another, and then me, pounding into her—more of a frenzy, more of a fuck. This isn't like that one bit. This is passionate and sweet. In fact, this isn't fucking at all.

I have my hands on her hips, helping her to grind her clit against my pelvis while I nuzzle her breasts, kissing and licking my way over every part of her body within reach. This is amazing, but with her sitting on top of me I can't kiss her very easily. While I'm deep inside her like this, I want to be devoting myself to her, and I can't very well do that if I can't even kiss her sweet mouth.

I pin her against me with one forearm, and while trying to keep my penis dutifully engaged, I adjust our position. I lay her back on the couch and position myself above her. Next, I swipe some of the cushions from behind us on to the floor to give us some more room. When I lower my mouth to hers, her hands go immediately to my face, holding me like she's afraid I'm not real, or that I'll disappear.

My body is cradled between her bent legs, but my penetration is limited, so I hook my arm under one of her knees and ease her thigh back toward her body. Right away, I'm able to get deeper inside her, then I pick up the pace a little.

When she begins moaning into my mouth, I increase the tempo of my thrusts and intertwine the fingers of one hand with hers. I guide our clasped hands above her head and over the arm of the couch. Our lips are perfectly in sync while I'm thrusting and grinding into her. With so many points of connection between us, it feels like we have a much deeper bond than just sex.

Her moaning gives way to an erotic whining that tightens my balls, "Oh, Salinger. You're so good, awwww... yes...awwww." And then her erotic whining turns into a whisper against my ear, "Salinger, you're going to make me come again.... I'm gonna... come..."

"Ok Baby, let go," I whisper back into her own ear.

She breaks all around me while I give her a few more strokes, fast and deep and then follow her over the cliff.

After collapsing on her, mingling our sweat, and eventually catching my breath, I notice she is hugging me against her body, and in no hurry for me to get off. Worried I must feel like a downed tree on top of her, I roll to my side, pushing her closer to the edge of the couch in the process. Then I reach over her body and scoop her tightly against me, so she doesn't fall off the edge. I rest my head on the arm of the sofa, and she nuzzles into me, her soft breath grazing my neck. We are both spent, our legs a tangled labyrinth of exhausted limbs.

I don't think I've ever been this happy.

Chapter Twenty Five

Airport

The cell phone alarm wakes us both at the same time. Avery and I are still naked except for her thigh highs, and we are matted together like a single dreadlock.

"What the heck time is it?" I ask. It's still dark except for the bright light from the kitchen that's been left on.

"Time to get to the airport," she says, before kissing my neck and then nibbling on my earlobe.

Her tender lips make me groan, "Can't you skip it? It's only Christmas with your family." I drag my hand up the back of her thigh and along the straps of her garter.

"Do you think I should shower and wash the sex off of me? I think I'd rather skip it and stay here for ten extra minutes," she says quietly into the side of my face, which tickles down my ear canal and nudges my penis to attention.

"You better go get in the shower, I wouldn't be finished with you in ten minutes," I say, as I somewhat awkwardly lift myself over the top of her and walk toward the kitchen with my semi-hard cock starting to show off.

"I'll make you some coffee," I say over my shoulder. It's a better plan than sliding in the shower with her, she would definitely miss her flight in that case.

While she showers and gets ready, I make coffee and pick up our discarded clothing. My contacts are extended wear, but they feel like they've adhered to my eyeballs. I need to press my fingers into my eyelids and wiggle my eyes around just to make sure they are not, in fact, glued in place.

When she comes into the kitchen with a fresh face and towel-dried hair, I'm standing here wearing only my pants and handing her a mug of freshly brewed coffee with vanilla creamer from the fridge. I myself will not be drinking the coffee because I have every intention of falling onto my bed when I get home, and sleeping for the rest of the day.

She walks toward me, brings the mug to her lips and turns me around at the same time. Oh yeah, the scar, and just when I was starting to feel normal. Closing the space between us, she rests her cheek against my shoulder blade, right above the ragged scar that takes up half my back. I close my eyes and wonder what she's thinking. She sets the mug down on the counter, then wraps her left arm around me, splaying her open palm against my abdomen. Then she begins caressing my scar with her right hand.

It doesn't entirely feel like my skin, when she moves her palm over it, I'm aware she is touching me, I just can't really feel the contact. It's like touching a fireman through his bunker gear, he would feel it, but not really *feel* it. I would say at least three full minutes pass with her holding me and caressing my back, cheek still against my skin. I'm frozen in place. Is she disgusted? Turned off? Why won't she say anything?

"I knew I felt something last night," she says into my back. "Did this help mold you into the man you are today?"

I scoff, "Yeah, you could say that."

"Then I'm so grateful for this. It will remind me every day how lucky I am."

I don't even know what to say to that, as my mouth hangs limply open. It's the most remarkable twist anyone has ever put on my whole ordeal. After a moment, I turn around and collect her in my arms. For the first time in my life, the bitter hatred of my scar and everything it represents feels a little lighter, and I feel like less of a victim. I hang on to her for a long time waiting for the lump in my throat to dissolve so I can speak.

"I need to line up the Uber, or I'm going to miss my flight."

"Then miss it," I say, quietly into her apple-scented hair.

"I'm serious."

"Me too."

She leans back, gauging my level of seriousness.

"You don't need an Uber, I'll take you to the airport," is what I say out loud, what I say in my head is, *this is going to be the last Christmas we spend apart.*

Chapter Twenty Six

Work

Christmas comes and goes without newsworthy incident. The office is a ghost town because everyone is off until the second of January. I, however, have decided to work a few days inside that sweet spot between Christmas and New Year's, because Avery doesn't have a shift at the hospital until the fourth, so I'm taking the second and third off as well. To be perfectly honest though, I love how quiet it is around here. My productivity level has morphed into hyper speed, so I shouldn't need to come back until mid-January if I keep up this pace. Of course, I'll need to be back before then because Jessie and I already have two business trips on the calendar for January. Happy New Year, don't everyone try to sell your mineral rights all at once.

Avery and I have exchanged some pretty incredible sexts over the last few days, and two of the images are still on my phone. I'm keeping them because they don't show her face or otherwise identify her, but I did delete the others, after memorizing them, of course. The two that remain serve as masturbatory fodder while she's away. My favorite is a chest shot of her bare tits and an enormous, bulky necklace, the caption said, *look what Santa brought me.* The other photo still on my phone was taken in the mirror and shows her from the back. In it, she is wearing a Santa costume top and nothing else. She has the Santa jacket clutched tightly around her body, and the fluffy white trim at the base of the costume only covers about twenty-five percent of her ass. Her perfect…naked…ass. The caption said, *My brother, Ezra dressed up for my nieces and nephews and then left the costume evidence of their parent's betrayal in the downstairs bathroom.*

I have sent some pretty filthy text messages myself, but when she asked me to send her a sexy picture, I sent one of Nash wearing a tie. I'm not really a dick-pic kind of guy. Plus, when women send stuff like that, it's sexy as hell, but when guys do it, it comes off cheesy. I did take one though, just never sent it. In the picture I was bare-chested with my bottom half covered with a white sheet, you can't exactly see my cock, but the size and shape of it are clear as day. I may still send it tonight when I talk to her. In any event, she will be home tomorrow night, and we head to the cabin the following morning, New Year's Eve.

Avery is full of surprises. First, there was the garter belt for fondue, which by the way, leads me to believe her intention that night was seduction. Even long before she came across the dirty talk cards, her intent was clear. Then these beat-off texts. It all makes me think she is sexually adventurous and that is very exciting for me. Not that I would ever take her to 1462, but I think she would be up for it. I wouldn't want to share her with the club, even if I'm the only one that fucks her. I don't know how Silas does 1462 with Jessie. I must be way too possessive of what's mine because the desire to share that experience with her is nowhere near my radar. In fact, I would be happy never going to the club again.

Chapter Twenty Seven

Snow

There are several feet of snow in the mountains, and even though the roads are plowed, a four-wheel drive vehicle is all but mandatory. My Tahoe makes quick work of the snow even on the smaller, unplowed side roads. We have been off the highway for forty-five minutes already, so I'm starting to think the cabin is out in the middle of nowhere.

There is a heavy grayness in the low clouds that warn of incoming snow, making the sky feel like a giant cinder block in the air, just waiting to drop on your head. I know snow is forecasted for the duration of our stay, but I'm not too sure a blizzard isn't about to blow through this mountain canyon.

Incidentally, I brought enough food to see us through a blizzard but not because of the weather, it's because I wanted to have a bunch of options, and frankly, I didn't know what to get, so I bought it all.

The online pictures of the rental cabin look fantastic, but they don't paint the whole picture. For example, the cabin has a *full kitchen* but does that mean it has all the pots and pans necessary to cook in it? It also boasts a wood burning fireplace but neglects to mention if there is a stack of firewood laid out for our convenience. Anyway, the result of not having answers to all these questions has resulted in a fully stuffed SUV, and our ability to ride out a nuclear war or zombie apocalypse in well-fed comfort.

"It's starting to snow again, I hope you packed warm pajamas," I joke, as if she will even be wearing pajamas.

"I did," she winks. "It's going to be cold, I heard up to two more feet of snow."

"If it dumps that much, we might miss the New Year's fireworks in town," I say, as I take her hand and lace our fingers together.

"We won't be missing any fireworks," she says with authority, and I agree wholeheartedly with the assessment.

**

When we arrive, the cabin looks much like the online photos…if the online photos were taken thirty years ago. I was expecting something a little less rustic, and a little homier, maybe something with wood smoke drifting up from the chimney or a warm glow shining out from the windows onto the wraparound porch.

Well, there *is* a wraparound porch. Contrary to my vision, the cabin looks cold and closed up, and the stairs to the patio aren't even cleared of snow. For that matter, there aren't any footprints or snowshoe tracks' indicating anyone has even been by to check on the place. If it were me renting this cabin out to guests, the fireplace would be crackling, the lights would be on, and the stairs and path would be shoveled.

Avery lights up, "Salinger, this is a winter wonderland! It's perfect, we are surrounded by snow, and pine trees, and mountains…and look at the cabin!" She says all this with genuine excitement, which wipes at least a little of the disappointment off my face.

"It *is* a wonder all right. Let's go check it out before we unload anything," I say, as I open the door for Nash to go bounding off through the snow. He's never been in such deep snow so you would think he'd just fallen into a vat of filet mignon by his reaction. We both laugh at his frolicking, then I start to throw snowballs at him. He tries to catch them in his mouth, but they explode first and dust his face with powder.

I think, to stand up for my dog, Avery hits me in the side of the face with a snowball, which hits and then sprinkles icy snowflakes down my neck and into my unzipped coat. I turn slowly to look at her and her audacity, which is when I get hit with another incoming snowball. This woman definitely has three older brothers, because two snowballs to my face is a gutsy move.

Instead of reaching for a handful of snow to ball up into a weapon, I charge her. She squeals and tries to run, but the snow is up to her knees, so it slows her progress. I catch up to her in a few seconds, then playfully wrestle her to the ground, where we sink into the undisturbed majesty that is the snow-covered mountains.

We kiss like this for a long time considering how fucking cold it is, but the setting is spectacular and the snow is drifting down on us in big, fluffy clumps. When Nash comes over and starts to sniff and nudge our faces with his cold invasive nose, I stand up, tugging Avery with me.

We both look like powdered donuts as we make our way to the cabin, then climb the stairs before stomping the snow off our boots under the cover of the patio.

Nash trots around the other side of the patio exploring while I fish the keys out of my pocket, and unlock the front door. The first thing I notice when we walk in is that glaciers in the Arctic give off more heat, and the second thing is the huge, stacked stone hearth around the fireplace.

"It might be warmer if we dig an igloo out back," I say, noticing how I can see my breath even though I'm standing inside the cabin.

"I'll look for the thermostat," she says helpfully, then adds, "This place is amazing! I'm so happy to be here with you...even though you just rolled me in the snow like the base of a snowman."

I chuckle as I head straight to the fireplace intent on lighting a blazing fire. The cabin interior trumps its exterior by a mile and at least looks like it's from this decade, which is good because I was starting to worry that I didn't look closely enough at the online photos.

Inside, it has a cozier feel, current temperature notwithstanding. There is the monochromatic look of wood *everywhere*. There are wide planks of hand scraped hardwood covering the floors, walls, and ceilings, as well as large, rough-hewn ceiling timbers that all rise to meet the structural ridge beam running the length of the cabin.

The main living area with the fireplace has a russet colored leather sofa and loveseat that are studded with bronze nail heads around the trim. The furniture looks robust and expensive. There is also a sizeable brown and white cowhide rug on the floor in front of the fireplace. It doesn't bring to mind quite the same image as a bearskin rug for the eventual, if not mandatory, fuck in front of the roaring fire, but it looks cool. The other noteworthy feature is the antler chandelier hanging above the reclaimed wood coffee table. It's the kind of thing that would be hard to pull off anywhere except a mountain home, but again, really cool.

"I can't find a thermostat anywhere," Avery announces, as she brings her own heat into the room with her.

"That doesn't sound good does it?" I ask. "But I did find out why it's so damn cold in here. Someone left the flue to the fireplace open."

"Burrrrr," she wraps her arms around herself, then smiles a wide smile, "Come here, I want to show you something."

I follow her through the sliding barn door that evidently leads to the bedrooms.

"Isn't it perfect?" she gushes, while pointing at the massive, king-sized, four-poster bed made entirely of logs. It's covered with a heavy, multi-colored quilt that has a grandma's quilting circle look to it.

"Yeah, I pretty much want that bed in my house," I say, matching her smile. It's a rustic, behemoth of a bed—that we may need to pole-vault in to, but it redeems the owner for not having plowed us a path to the front door. As big as the bed is, there is still space in the room for a matching dresser, two nightstands, and another wood fireplace.

"The other bedroom has log bunk beds!" Avery says, already in love with the cabin.

"Perfect! I get top bunk though, because I get a little claustrophobic on the bottom sometimes," I wink at her, and then pull her in for a kiss on her cold lips.

"Then I'm sleeping on top bunk with you," she says with a wink of her own. I *cannot* wait to christen that huge bed with four days of unbridled sex, but right now, we need to get the heat on and the fire going.

There is a small pile of wood next to the hearth, along with some kindling but it won't last long, so Nash and I set out looking for the woodpile outside. We find it on the far side of the wraparound porch. The problem is that the logs are former tree trunks and have not been cut down at all, which explains the ax sticking out of the base log.

"I have to chop this wood like a fricken pioneer on the wild frontier if we want to have a fire," I say to Avery as she comes around the corner.

"Well, pioneer up, because I found the thermostat...but it's broken."

"Come again?" I say. That can't be possible...in the snowy mountains...during blizzard conditions.

"Yeah, it's broken. I can't even get it to turn on, but the dial is set to 68."

"I'll look at it. Hopefully it's not really broken, or I'll be out here chopping wood all night."

***

As it turns out, the thermostat isn't broken at all—the furnace is. This is problematic for a myriad of reasons, one, we have no cell service to call the owner or anyone else, two, we are about to get a couple more feet of snow, and three, it's fucking cold. I'm thinking the furnace crapped out recently though because mercifully, none of the pipes have burst.

By the time we unload the Tahoe, the fire has warmed the place to a tolerable level, and Nash is lying on his bed refusing to come with me to tend to the lumberjack duties.

"Come on, you look like Babe, my trusty Blue Ox, why don't you act like it?" I ask him while trying to coax him up from his bed in the corner.

"Sorry, Paul Bunyan, looks like he's sticking with me," Avery says as she smiles at me from the kitchen where she is putting the food away. The cabin has an open concept, with the kitchen overlooking both the living room and the small dining table with four chairs. It's perfect.

"I hate to say it, but I think we are going to need to close off the bedrooms and keep the heat in here," I say, realizing why the heavy sliding barn door is there. Turns out it's not just for aesthetics.

After sparing a thought for that amazing log bed, I add, "For now anyway. We also need to leave the bathroom door open. That way the heat from in here will help to preserve the pipes in there. I'm sure they are insulated really well, but I don't want to take the chance of an even bigger problem," I say this as I suit up in my coat and boots, preparing to go outside and face the chopping block.

"Ok, I'll hold down the fort in here with Nash," Avery says, then adds, "At least there is no danger of running out of food."

***

I haven't chopped wood in ages, and even then it was only for a campfire, not at all the quantity needed here for the next few days. Before long, I have to take my coat off, because the exertion is keeping me plenty warm. Swinging an ax, turns out, is a decent workout.

The contrast of my body heat against the sharp, cold air getting sucked into my lungs makes me feel hardy and invigorated, and steam is literally rising off my sweaty body. I have no idea how much wood we will need, but I'd rather chop a ton now rather than having to do it again later. Turns out, frontier living isn't for pussies.

It takes only one trip inside with an armful of firewood for Avery to catch my attention. She is standing in the kitchen wearing white long underwear, fluffy boot-style slippers, and an oversized sweatshirt. I take the chopped wood over to the big, stone hearth, add another log to the fire, and then make my way to the kitchen.

"Look at you, all rugged and sexy!" she fans herself with her hand, then adds, "I made us a little lunch, are you hungry?"

"It just so happens that I *am* hungry," I say, as I close in on her. My lips find hers while I slide my hands up inside her sweatshirt.

She yelps, and then laughs, "Your hands are freezing!" Then her mouth is back on mine.

"That's funny because the rest of me feels very, very hot," I say. I discover right away she is not wearing a bra, and when my cold fingers find her nipples, she exhales a moan. The contrast of her warm breasts against my ice cold hands must feel electric for her as I strum my fingers over her tight nipples. She's almost breathless against my mouth she is so turned on by the nipple tweaking.

I turn her around to face the counter, and then slide one hand down the front of her thermal underwear and then between her legs. My fingers find her warm pussy lips and spread them open with two cold fingers. I lean in and speak slowly and deliberately soft into her ear, "Thanks for the lunch, but the only thing I'm hungry for right now is your silky, wet pussy."

"Oh, my Gaud!" she groans.

"What do you think? Would you like to feel my wet tongue against this needy little clit right here?" As I reference her clit, I wiggle one frosty digit against it, making her gasp.

"Salinger, all I can think about right now is your mouth on my pussy," she says with breathless impatience. My chilled fingers still hold her open and have not moved except for the few seconds against her clit. This leaves her feeling open and ready, but so far, unfulfilled.

I withdraw my hand from down her pants and let go of her straining nipple to lift her sweatshirt off. Even with the smoldering heat of her body, my hands still feel like two blocks of ice, but I'm trying to keep them to her erogenous zones, so she doesn't feel cold once I get her naked. Which needs to happen soon or my cock is going to rip through these jeans. I lightly drag the fingers of one hand down her body, from the back of her neck to the waistline of her long underwear, then I speak against her ear again. My voice comes off menacing and cruel, "You have five seconds to get these off, or I'm going to rip them off of you."

She hooks her thumbs into the elastic but when she pushes them down she doesn't bend or lift her legs, she bends over all the way and presents herself to me like that. Then she steps out of the slippers and long underwear one leg at a time. I can see plainly how wet her pussy is, but as much as I want to bury my face in it, the position and angle are all wrong.

Her legs are spread at this point, and she's bent all the way over when she reaches between her legs and starts to play with herself, "Can you see how bad I want you, Salinger? I'm so wet. I can't wait to feel your big, hard cock inside me," as she says this, she slips a finger into her pussy and I almost jizz in my pants it's so hot.

"Get on the counter," I demand, as I strip off my shirt and unbutton a few buttons of my jeans. She climbs up and is now on her knees with her forearms resting against the raised bar-top portion of the counter. She's over-looking the living room and facing the fireplace now. The way her ass is displayed and her pussy is cradled between her thighs flips a primal switch inside me as I step forward.

"Widen your knees," I direct. She does, and her pussy comes more into view as she arches her back for my benefit.

"Wider."

She does, now her legs are wrenched open, and her vagina is literally presented to me. I feel like I'm vibrating from the inside, humming with the need to have her. I reach between her spread legs and caress her lips, moistening my fingers and then finding her clit.

"Your cold fingers feel so good against my clit," she whisper-moans. I start to rub small circles against it, then bend forward and put my mouth on her. I fucking can't get enough of her taste as I lick and stroke her heat while rubbing her clitoris. Something about seeing her finger herself a minute ago makes me want to watch my own finger slide in and out of her. I want to see how her pussy clings to me and how much my finger glistens from being inside her.

I switch hands for rubbing her clit and slowly advance two fingers inside her phenomenal pussy. Her body clamps around my fingers and then almost sucks them as I slide them slowly out. It's exactly how she feels on my cock, but this time I'm so close I can smell her, and see the shiny rawness between her pussy lips.

"Turn around," I rasp.

"Thank God! My knees are killing me," she giggles, as she turns over. Now her elbows are leaning back against the raised bar-top, and her ass is on the counter. "Did you like watching your fingers plunge in and out of my pussy?" she asks. Every single time she says pussy, it sounds like the hottest thing I have ever heard in my life.

"Yeah, I did." I look at her dubiously, as her fingers find her slick opening again.

"Well then... I want you to watch some more," she says this with a crafty smile on her face. "Do you know I touched myself while I watched you chop wood from the bedroom window?" she asks coyly, fingers sliding all the way out, then back in.

I shake my head slowly.

"I did. You were *so...unbelievably...sexy*, that I couldn't keep my hands off myself." Then she brings her dewy fingers up to her nipple. After spreading her juices around the tip, she starts to roll it between finger and thumb. "You looked so handsome and manly out there, that I almost couldn't believe you were mine." I'm dumbfounded by this statement because I feel the same way when I look at her, *I can't believe she's mine*.

I don't say anything, I just watch her as my feral nature begins to tighten its grip on my balls.

"So, I had to touch myself," she smiles wickedly and I return the look. "I did it just like this," she gives her nipple a tug before dropping her fingers to her vagina. She spreads open her legs even more and then starts to rub her clit. The whole thing is so hot I couldn't tear my eyes off of her if my life depended on it.

"Take off your pants, I have to see your beautiful cock while I stroke my pussy."

175

In what feels like slow motion, I take off my boots, jeans, and boxer-briefs. My dick is protruding from my body like the unrestrained appendage that it is.

"When you were playing with yourself, did you imagine me fucking you? Or going down on you?" I ask as I take a step closer.

"You were fu—"

That's all the information I need before burying my cock in her. The sensation is like nothing I have ever felt before. Then realization slaps me in the face, and I pull out of her body. "I need to get a condom."

"It's ok. I have an IUD," she says.

It's only a millisecond before my entire shaft is snug in her delicious grip. This is the first time I've had sex without a condom since high school, and I'm dizzy with the intensity of it. I pull her off the counter, and she wraps her arms and legs around me. The feel of her naked vagina against my bare cock is so insane that if I don't control the depth and speed of our fucking, I'm going to spout off way too soon.

I walk over to the barn door and slide it open, the feel of the cold air envelops us, but I don't care because there is enough body heat between us to light a tinder fire. My penis slides out as I put her down on the bed. The loss of warmth and tightness around my cock feels like a severed arm as the cold settles around the dampness of me. I back her up on the bed while crawling forward on top of her.

"I'm going to fuck you so well, your panties will get wet next week just thinking about it," I say, as she nods enthusiastically. This time when I press tightly into her I take her nipple in my mouth, sucking it first, then flicking it with my tongue as she deeply arches her back.

"I love when you do that to my nipples, oh God, I could get off with just your mouth on my tits. But your cock...the way you...how you...ohhhh, yeah that."

After a while, I can tell she is trying to delay her orgasm, and I've already backed myself off as much as I can, this just may be a runaway train until I get used to skin on skin sex. I lean down to her mouth and kiss her gently, as I slow my thrust even more.

"Do you have any idea what you've done to me?" I ask before we dissolve into an even deeper kiss. What *has* she done to me? Why does everything feel so natural and effortless with her?

I was so devastated by Jessie, I thought it would take a long time to put the pieces of myself back together, but oddly enough, I don't have to put myself back together at all. In fact, I was never broken. I was on the wrong path. Having the door slammed shut in my face was what I needed to right my compass. All the loss and anguish I felt was me hanging on to something that wasn't right in the first place. Now that I'm free of those burdens, my sites have been realigned. I think I was waiting for Avery.

It's freezing in this room, and her nipples are like marbles against my chest, which along with her clenched pussy, is what pushes me over the ledge. I spurt heavy surges of cum right into her vagina before thinking better of it, but she is lost in her own release, so I'm not even sure she notices.

After a bit, I roll her on top of me, so I'm not crushing her, and she lays her cheek against my chest. The quilt feels like I've rolled over onto a sheet of ice, but I want to stay right here, just like this.

"Do you have any idea what you've done to *me*?" she whispers, then I'm pretty sure I feel a tear hit my chest. I don't want to address the fact she is crying in here because our sweat is turning cold and clammy in the frozen tundra of the cabin bedroom. I grab one side of the heavy quilt and attempt to cover us with it, but its own exposure to the elements only surrounds us with the chill of winter.

"We've got to get out of this room," I announce, as I feel her start to shiver.

"I can think of worse ways to go than freezing to death while pressed up against your naked, tattooed, perfect body," she says, quietly against my skin.

Chapter Twenty Eight

Fireplace

I step back into my jeans and then immediately go add a couple of logs to the fire. Avery pulls her sweatshirt over her head and for that split second before it slides over her naked tits, I'm completely entranced by them. Even after the sweatshirt is on, it only *just* covers her ass, leaving her bare legs to tempt me.

Wanting to recreate the position we were in before the freeze out, I lie back on the couch and bring her with me. This time, her face is tucked into my neck instead of on my chest, so the perfect placement of my hands is just under the grey fleece on her panty-less ass.

I wonder what the record number of times you could fuck someone in a day is? I feel like my cock could get hard fifty times, fuck her breathless and still fill up for the fifty-first round. Her butt is still a little cold, but her flawless skin warms beneath my hands. I have an incredible urge to smack dat ass, but doing that may take the sincerity out of my question.

"Aves, why the tears? Did I do something?" I ask, as I consciously tell myself to loosen my grip on her ripe booty.

"Did you do something?" she asks, before burying her face deeper into the side of my neck and exhaling long and slow. "Yeah, I'd say you did something."

179

I pause and wait for her to go on, which she doesn't do right away. I feel a very light shudder run through her, and I realize she is crying for real now, not just a stray tear. I respectfully remove my hands from her butt and hug her against me instead. I think there is more to the story about why she left her fiancé and moved here than she has let on, but I'm not going to push her to tell me. I bring one hand up to cradle her head and firm up my hug, I want her to know I'm here to comfort her as long as she needs me to.

"For one thing, you've taught me a lot," she says. I don't know what she means by that, so I wait for her to go on.

"You've taught me how it's supposed to feel," she says, with no elaboration at all. Entire minutes tick by before she goes on, "I've never had that before, and it's new, and—and I like it."

"Did he hurt you?" I ask. So much for not being pushy.

"No," she says flatly. I'm relieved to hear that because I'm not too sure what I would do. Actually, I do know what I would do, and he would probably end up in the hospital. I have no tolerance for men that mistreat their women. It's such a place of honor to be able to love and protect your girl. Anyone who doesn't acknowledge that basic fact, shouldn't have a partner, period.

"Not physically anyway," she adds, and all of the air in my balloon whooshes out all at once. I forgot, there are many ways to mistreat someone, perhaps a trip to Seattle is in my future after all. I want to ask her, *How*? Because I can't force that information to compute. She is so amazing, how could someone not recognize that? I can feel my face heating up and my jaw tightening, but I'm careful not to speak, not yet.

"He has a problem with alcohol, and I think, with anger too," she says, and it comes out timid like she's trying to protect him. I pull back and kiss her head because if I say anything, it will spook her and she won't divulge anything else about it.

"He's not what you typically think of when you hear the term alcoholic. He didn't wake up in the gutter, he didn't drink all day long, and he's the CFO of a massive company—how can someone who gets up and goes to work every day be an alcoholic? Alcoholics shouldn't be able to hold brilliant positions in Fortune 500 companies," her voice has gained strength, it's obvious there is anger covering a mountain of hurt.

"There is a term for people like that. They are called functioning alcoholics, Aves. In fact, they make up the majority of alcoholics out there. Functioning in day to day life doesn't mean they can't still have a drinking problem."

"I know that now. The problem wasn't even necessarily when he was drinking. I mean, that *was* a problem, he would become very sloppy, and he turned into someone I didn't respect anymore. But the other component people don't understand is how they behave when they are *not* drinking. For him, it was like he needed to be feeding that addiction, and if he wasn't, he was very angry and aggressive."

"There is a term for that too, it's called being a dry drunk," I say, "Here's the thing though, for the most part, they are good people. It's a disease," I have too much first-hand knowledge of this fact to not mention it. My dad was an alcoholic. He passed away more than a decade ago, but his alcoholism still left an indelible mark across my family.

"He is a good person, that's why I stayed with him for so long. His drinking was very cyclical, so we went through that crazy pattern for years and years. He would get in a pattern of drinking too much, then inevitably do something mean or stupid. He would always feel terrible about it and become very contrite. Then he would make all kinds of promises about slowing down or stopping altogether. Then eventually— ever so gently, he would start drinking again, and the cycle would repeat. It would have repeated forever too, that's why I had to extricate myself."

"My dad used to say those slides, the easing right back into drinking again, were from a microscopic seed that grew by tiny increments, eventually growing into something that would tell him one sip wouldn't hurt, or one beer after all this time wouldn't be enough to knock him off his stride. It always did though." I'm surprised I'm talking about my dad. I haven't shared the fact that he was an alcoholic with anyone. Ever.

Avery pulls back to look at my face. She must be realizing all my knowledge on the topic came at a heavy price. She lays her head on my chest and begins tracing the names sewn into my ribs with ink.

"Salinger, you've been through so much. How has life not destroyed you? How are you such an amazing person after facing so much adversity?"

"Life has destroyed me," I say flatly, "But things are on the upswing now." I smile to myself when I realize the truth behind my statement.

"You're like a Phoenix, rising from the ashes," she says, as she kisses my chest. She doesn't stop her reverent tracing of the names, it's like she is paying her respects to those men. The undercurrent created by such a meaningful act hitches in my throat. I have to hold my breath to steady my emotions, every one of those guys should be at my wedding. The sense of loss I feel for them is such a cold, uninhabitable place. It crushes me under the weight of an orbiting planet, and it steals my breath.

I feel tears streak across my temples and try to pool in my ears. I've opened the door on thoughts of my buddies, and I can't shut it. It's like a heard of wildebeests are charging through the doorway preventing me from closing it and locking it up tight.

"I am," I say, managing to only sound a little choked up. "A Phoenix, rising from the ashes. That's what this tattoo signifies to me," I say as I point to my right bicep, which is currently around her back. As bold and prominent as the tattoo is, and as much as I wanted it to, I've never really felt like it represented me. Maybe the flames, but I've never really identified with the rising Phoenix.

"What about this one?" she asks, as she tries to pronounce the phrase. "Lux in Tenebris—is that how you say it?"

"It's Latin for *Light in the Darkness*," I say. Her chin is against my chest, while she studies the chaos of ink on my arm, waiting for me to elaborate. I guess a guided tour of my tattoos is a good way to cut right through to my soul. I hope she has braced herself because every single drop of ink on my arms means something to me, and most of them were not laid down in sweetness and light. "Because I always strive to be the light in the darkness. It's a reminder that the world can be dark and ruthless, but I can still choose to believe in the inherent good out there."

"You *are* a light in the darkness. That is perfect for you. What about this one?"

"The anchor?" I ask, "That symbolizes strength and stability, and usually something or *someone* that holds you in place. You know, providing the strength to hold on, no matter how tough life may get."

"Is your anchor a person or a thing?" she asks. I have to stop and think for a bit because Jessie has always been that anchor for me, but perhaps the designation was cast prematurely, or maybe people's anchors change throughout their life. I don't really know how to answer her, so I go for vague, "I think it has always been people, but I suppose throughout life, anchors can shift or be thrown into fresh water."

She squirms up my body and kisses my mouth while she holds one side of my face in her hand. Then she pulls back a millimeter and whispers, "I want to be your anchor."

That's it. She really is perfect for me. My hands find her ass again then slide up the back of her sweatshirt. Her skin is soft, the crackling of the fire is soothing, and her mouth on mine—the whole thing is so emotional and so damn sensual.

"And I want to be yours," I mumble between our shifting mouths.

After a while, she starts to kiss her way down my neck and then to my other arm of tattoos. "I want to know more about you," she says playfully, even though there is nothing playful to be unearthed in any of my tattoos. She points to a symbol, "This one. It's little, but I bet it has big significance for you."

"That is a semi-colon," I say, even though that much is obvious. "You know how a semi-colon indicates a pause in a sentence, but not a hard stop like a period?"

"Yes," she says as she sits up with her knees on either side of my hips. She is straddling me, and she's not wearing any panties. The sweatshirt conceals her, but only just. "Go on," she prompts.

183

"Sometimes life feels like a hard stop, but then you make the choice to go on." I'm trying to get a glimpse between her legs, but the sweatshirt serves as a swatch of cock-block. "There was a time in my life where I thought I was at the end of my story. I couldn't understand why I had lived through the explosion when everyone else died. And I couldn't find any meaning in life beyond my suffering. Those were some very dark months for me while my body healed," I say.

"But then you chose to continue on," she finishes for me.

"Exactly."

She brings her palm to her chest, and it looks like she is a little choked up. "Thank you—for choosing to go on." Then her eyes well up with tears. The sentiment between us merged with the emotion I feel just thinking about those days, is enough to fill my eyes with tears too. Jesus Christ, did I get a shot of estrogen or something? Why am I so emotional?

To spare me from myself, she points to another tattoo, "This is for the Marines, right?"

"Yep, that's the Marine Corps emblem," I say about the eagle, globe and anchor tattoo.

"Semper Fidelis," she muses to herself. "That means always faithful, right?" I nod while she studies the image and traces the eagle's wings with the tip of her finger, which is intensely ticklish on the inside of my tricep where the emblem resides. "What does zero-three-one-one mean?"

"It's, Oh three eleven, and it's my military occupational specialty. MOS 0311 designates me as a Rifleman in the United States Marine Corps."

"God-Damn, that's sexy!" she says with a huge grin that I mirror at once.

"Oorah!"

"What about this one?" she asks, "Aut inveniam viam aut faciam? Latin too I presume?"

"I like to be mysterious with the Latin phrases. That way people don't know everything about me. I could tell you it meant, *I hate when sweatshirts get in the way of my amazing view*, and you would have to believe that because you probably don't read Latin."

"This view?" she asks as she raises her sweatshirt up a few inches. Her naked pussy is sitting on the row of buttons on the fly of my jeans.

I can't even respond to her question, but I do find her clitoris with my thumb.

"Mmmmmm," she mumbles as she smiles and lolls her head back.

"It means, *I shall either find a way, or I will make one*," I finally say, even though I am hugely distracted by her precocious clit.

"I like the sound of that," she says with the sexiest little rasp to her voice. Then she pulls the sweatshirt all the way over her head and drops it to the floor. She has the most perfect tits, and now I can unabashedly stare at them because her eyes are closed, and her head is rocked back.

The thought of her getting wet against the crotch of my jeans is hot enough to commit me to bringing her to orgasm just like this. As it is, every time I button or unbutton these jeans I'm going to think about her wet pussy on them.

She starts to ride me a little, and I'm sure my erection is pressing the buttons of my jeans against her. Her rocking motion has me so entranced by the movement of her tits that I can't look at anything else.

It's not until long after her titty quivering orgasm that I realize how lucky I am that she didn't ask me about Aiden's tattoo. I don't talk about that tattoo with anyone, it still feels too raw, even after all these years.

"I made us a snack before you distracted me so thoroughly. It's been awhile, do you think we can still eat it?"

"Let's go look. I'm fucking starving."

Chapter Twenty Nine

Snowshoes

We head to the kitchen where Avery had prepared a very nice looking snack tray. There is cheese, salami, crackers, grapes, and olives—and it would have been delicious two hours ago. Now the cheese has hardened, and the salami has wilted and somehow started to sweat.

"Well," she sighs, "The grapes still look good."

"Don't forget about the crackers," I add with a wry smile.

Avery tugs her sweatshirt down over her ass and then hops up on the counter before grabbing a handful of grapes. I decide to open a bottle of wine before I realize I forgot to bring a wine opener. I rifle through the cabinets looking for one while Avery muses about Nash.

"He is such a chill dog."

"He's just happy to be here," I say, then celebrate finding a wine opener by throwing my arms up in the air, "Success!"

"What time is it anyway? We have to keep our eye on the time, so we don't miss the New Year," she says before popping a grape into her mouth.

I glance at my watch, "It's not quite four o'clock, I think we're still good. We are not yet in danger of missing the stroke of midnight."

"I'm gonna stroke you at midnight," she says in a ridiculous attempt at a come-back.

"Yeah, see that you do," I say as I approach her with a chilled glass of something white that the guy at the liquor store said was a real crowd pleaser. I'm more of a beer guy, myself. I like wine, just not enough to be familiar with all the varietals or their particular tasting notes, or aromatic intensities. The only thing I considered before opening the white instead of the red, is the fact that we will have champagne for New Year's, and it would probably piggyback better with the white.

"This is perfect. A chilled glass of wine by the crackling fire, with the man of my dreams—" she only stops talking because I've descended on her mouth. She just referred to me as the man of her dreams, and the designation swells my crystallized heart. If someone as broken as I am can be the man of someone's dreams, then there is hope in this world yet.

"Mmmm, you taste like wine," then she snorts and starts laughing, "...And I want to get drunk," she finishes, while still laughing at herself.

"It's just you and me, Baby, and I brought enough alcohol to do the trick," I say, then inwardly cringe. How could I say that after what she shared with me today?

Thankfully, she doesn't seem to notice, "Well then, lock the doors, because I-am-in." She is still giggling when she adds, "Are you sure you're not stoned? Your eyes are really red."

"I was wondering about that, my contacts are bothering me, I'm thinking of taking them out."

"I bet it's the fire. You should take them out though because you look dead-sexy in your glasses."

When I come back, less two contact lenses, she has taken a couple steaks out of the refrigerator, "Do you think we can fire up that grill?"

"I'm hoping so, I'll go check the propane," I offer.

"You know, we never did talk about this one," Avery says as she rests her hand on Aiden's tattoo. "And it's my favorite."

I'm quiet for a minute while my throat dries out and renders me unable to speak. So much for dodging that bullet. "I don't like to talk about that one," I finally say. There is a flash of disappointment that runs across her face, and it breaks my heart. Me not wanting to talk about it has nothing to do with trust, or not caring about her enough, or anything like that. It's just so intensely personal. It's a heavy, jagged cross that I have had to bear all of my adult life, and I've always carried it by myself. It's almost like introducing someone else to that compartment of my heart would weaken the bond I have with him.

"I'm sorry, I—"

"It's ok, Salinger. You don't have to apologize. I understand having things in the past that are hard to talk about. You are allowed to keep personal stuff to yourself," she says, she's being so understanding it makes me feel worse for not allowing her in.

"It's just that, I don't really—"

"Stop." She wraps her legs around my waist and pulls me in. "I need to be kissed by you while you're wearing those glasses."

***

By the time we grill steaks and eat dinner, it's almost eight o'clock before we venture outside to take Nash for a walk. I found some snowshoes in the coat closet earlier when I hung up our coats, but with the amount of snow on the ground, it's still hard for Nash to tramp through the snow drifts. It stopped snowing a couple of hours ago and apparently the front has moved on because the sky has opened up to showcase the entire universe.

"Look at the stars!" Avery shouts with unrestrained glee.

"It's incredible, right? Once you get away from all the city lights, it's like Heaven opens up."

"Salinger! I have never seen so many stars! And they look so close it's like you can reach out and touch them!" she says this while reaching out her hand, as though the stars really are within reach. She is completely astonished by the sky, and her excitement is infectious.

I have seen this view of the stars at least fifty times. It's still beautiful, but it's less shocking for me. I used to come to the mountains all the time with nothing but an ILBE pack and hike into the middle of nowhere when I needed to get away from everything. I would hike until exhaustion hit, then usually crumble to the ground and scream my throat raw. It was the only way I could purge the hell from my body, and it probably kept me from putting a gun in my mouth.

Nash is frolicking around like the show pony he is. The freedom of being off the leash is apparently equivalent to me hitting the mega-millions jackpot. He has developed this funny habit where he digs his nose into the snow, and then flops forward in some sort of dog summersault, then squirms on his back for a bit before jumping up and bounding off ahead of us.

We trudge through the snow for a long time, taking in the majesty of the night and talking about everything, from our childhoods to politics and then circling back around to growing up. It's a perfect night, with the white snow and the brilliant stars, it's almost like it's not even full dark out.

When we come to a steep downhill, Avery looks at me, "Looks like this is a good place to turn around."

"What?! Hills are the best part of snowshoeing. Going downhill anyway."

"We are going down there? It looks kinda steep," she says, her cheeks and nose are red from the cold, and she looks nervous.

"Yes! Well... only if you want to," I say, then add with excitement, "It's so fun! You just take a big dramatic step like you are walking off a ledge, then you keep doing it, and you're down the whole hill in like five steps."

"Ok, let's do it," she says, and I can see the little sister with three older brothers come out in her.

I call Nash over, then look at her to see if she has changed her mind. She has a fierce look of determination on her face, so I ask, "Ready?"

"Yep. Let's go." Then the two of us, plus Nash take off down the hill in a dust storm of snow.

As promised, we are down the hill in record time, laughing with the rush of adrenaline.

"That. Was. Awesome!" she says, then, "Let's do it again."

"You might change your mind after dragging your ass back up that hill," I say, still grinning like a little kid.

"I don't care," she says, then takes off running back up the hill. I'd say she loses her steam about a quarter of the way up as she slows her charge. "It's a little different going back up," she pants while looking over at me.

"I know. What takes ten steps to get down, takes seventy thousand to get back up," I say. Even so, we charge down the hill a second time and then drag our asses back up the hill again before we flop down in the snow like two panting snow angles.

"This is the best night of my life," Avery says, with her arms flung out to the sides. She is drinking in the view and indifferent to the temperature, just like me.

"Me too," I say as I turn to look at her pink-cheeked face.

***

As we hike back to the cabin in companionable silence, I say, "The tattoo is for someone I loved and lost. It was a long time ago." She looks over at me, and then quickly back down to her snowshoes, I recognize the tactic. It's so she doesn't inadvertently give off the wrong cue, and spook me back into silence.

"It's a Celtic cross. The knots symbolize the link between the physical and the spiritual world, and the loops represent the never-ending circle of existence." I'm quiet for a minute, trying to decide whether or not to tell her the rest.

"Salinger, that tattoo is a beautiful tribute to that person." She takes my hand, and we walk in silence for a few more minutes.

Then I speak again, "Semper mecum ad rursus conventum nostrum, is Latin for, *Forever with me until we meet again.*"

Chapter Thirty

Hearth

The rest of the way back to the cabin is mostly quiet, she doesn't want to pry, and I don't want to divulge any more information behind the significance of my tattoo. The result is that neither of us quite knows what to say. It's a comfortable silence though, the space between us doesn't need to be filled with words she's grasping for, or ones I'm tamping further down.

We are holding hands as we tromp through the deep snow, having left our energy behind us in our snowshoe tracks. Well, Nash's fireball of energy doesn't seem to be affected, he's acting like a kid at the fair who just fell into a cotton candy machine. I look at his lolling tongue and bubble-headed face and feel the need to remind him of something. "You know you're not a Husky, Right?" His ears go up, but it's more as a courtesy to me than any real understanding.

Once we get to the cabin and trudge up the stairs to the patio, we both unhook our snowshoes and stomp the snow off our boots.

"I'm going to bring the rest of this firewood in and stack it by the hearth, so we have it on hand. Go ahead in and warm up. Or don't, I can help you with that when I'm done." I wiggle my eyebrows at her, but I'm not too sure they even move because my face is so cold.

"Yeah, see that you do," she winks.

***

When I step inside with an armful of firewood, my glasses immediately fog up, requiring some stealth to get to the hearth without bumping into stuff. I didn't think to pack another set of contacts, and the ones I have with me are too irritating to put back in, so I'll have to deal with the nuisance of glasses. People think the thick, dark frames are some sort of fashion statement and Jessie calls them my urban hipster panty droppers, but the fact is, my vision is not my strongest asset.

It takes four trips to get all the wood I chopped earlier inside, and that's with huge armfuls, but the fire is chewing through them at a steady rate. If we don't keep it fed, we will get cold pretty quick. Nash is already passed out on his bed exhausted by the time I shrug out of my coat and pull off my hat.

When I turn around, I'm stunned by what I see. Avery is standing there wearing the hottest thing I have ever seen in my life. She is wearing a black, lacy, see-through outfit that looks like it would disintegrate if it got wet. The skirt is maybe four inches long—so to call it a skirt is a bit of a misnomer—and the top is like a long bra that covers her ribs too, but at the same time doesn't cover *anything*. It looks frilly but also hard and commanding.

"You look sexy as fuck!"

"And you, in those glasses with your hair all crazy, how am I supposed to keep my hands off of you?"

"I can't promise that outfit will make it out of here, it looks pretty delicate," I warn. For someone who wants to charge her, and fuck her until sparks are shooting out of her fingers and toes, I'm sure bolted to the ground. She is just full of surprises now, isn't she?

"Come here," I say, and it doesn't sound at all polite. She saunters up to me but remains just out of reach, so I close the gap in a microsecond. It takes every bit of my restraint not to rip this lace off and plow into her. Instead, I kiss her, almost gently, and caress her with hands that defy my lascivious intent. I tug my shirt over my head and almost lose my glasses in the frenzy, then I let go of her to clumsily step out of my boots and pop open the buttons on my fly.

"I want to play our game…I can't only wear this for five minutes," she says, to the ceiling.

I disengage from her neck and ask, "What?" I thought that was the point of the outfit, you know, to snare me into sex. Well, I'm snared.

"I want you to enjoy it a little more," she says while she runs her fingernails down my chest to the top of my jeans. They are unbuttoned and slung low on my hips so when she moves her fingertips just inside and tickles around my waist, my cock swells even more. It's beyond uncomfortable to have this big of a hard-on still harnessed inside my jeans, but I play along anyway.

"And which game would you be talking about, Avery?"

She laughs and slides her hands down the back of my jeans to clutch my ass, "The dice game."

"You know you can only tempt a bull for so long before he charges," I say with a sly grin on my face. I will humor her for a while, but I have no intention of playing games all night.

"Ok, let's bring some pillows and blankets out here in front of the fire so we can get nice and cozy," she says as she turns to walk toward the bedroom, showcasing her partially covered ass.

"We'll get nice and cozy alright," I say, dripping lecherous intent.

When she looks over her shoulder at me, she must see my shoulders squared, and my tightly wound body ready to pounce on her, because she pops her ass out and slowly rotates it one way, then back.

"I want you to do that again when you're sitting on my face, you dirty little tease." I feel like a beast, so I want to take her down and ravage the shit out of her. I'm all done with pleasantries, it's time to open her up.

"You want me to do what on your face? This?" Then she does her little hip rotation again, but deeper, and with her legs spread more. Fuck. That ass.

In four long strides, I'm behind her with one hand on her belly, preventing her from moving forward and the other forcefully gripping her mostly uncovered ass, "Are you sure you want to tease me like that?"

"Yeah, Salinger. First I'm going to tease you, then I'm going to submit to being your little plaything," she says as she twirks her ass against my hand and unbuttoned fly. "I'm going to let you do *anything* you want to me, no matter how filthy or depraved it might be."

My heart is pumping so hard I can feel the rocking in my throat at this point. If I don't fuck her soon, I will have no blood left to circulate the oxygen in my body. My cock is bursting full, and I feel like a caged animal. Let me do whatever I want? Shit, at this point I'm going to come as soon as my dick gets wet.

"You may regret those words. Now, go get the champagne while I get the pillows and blankets." Yep, it's time to get this ball rolling.

***

She's putting on a show with each and every move she makes as she sets up the fuck nest in front of the fireplace. I already moved the coffee table to make room for said fuck nest, and I put it in between us and Nash because the dog is not going to want to see this. My other contribution to game night is that I've opened the package of dice, which I'm now studying just to distract my dick from Avery's bent over stance. Like I said, she is very calculating while she prepares our bed on the floor.

This Goddamned, time-wasting game here consists of two action dice, two with body parts, and one with increments of time. Without wasting any more time with the superfluous directions, I assume you roll them all and end up with a time frame, two actions and two body parts. Or maybe you pick the action from the two or pick which body part, I don't fuckin know.

She crawls over between my legs, then gets up on her knees while she gathers up all her hair into a ponytail holder. For some reason, the motion of collecting her hair and bunching it all up arches her back and presses her tits out a little. I can see her tightened nipples rubbing against the rough lace and have an intense desire to suck them, right through the material, soaking the fabric as I pull her nipples into my mouth.

"Shall we get started?" she asks.

I nod. It's a slow, meticulous nod because it's all I can muster while trying not to pounce on her like a savage. If I grabbed the delicate fabric right between her tits, I would hardly have to tug, the lace would disintegrate in my hand.

"So, there are two dice for actions, and two for body parts, one of each are tame, the others, not so much."

"Ok, ladies first," I say. I'm eager and starting to unravel here.

"I'll just pick one of each without looking, and we will have to wait and see if they are tame or naughty."

I slide off the couch, dick preceding me the whole way, to sit next to her on the floor where our backs can lean up against the sofa. She mindlessly puts two dice to the side then drops the remaining ones between us. Thirty seconds, suck, and lips. For the record, I think *lips* should be up to the player's discretion, so if this were my roll, I'd already be between her thighs.

"Alright, set the timer," she says as she saddles up, placing one knee on either side of my lap. She leans in for a kiss while cupping my jaw with both of her hands. What starts off pretty PG, ratchets up in intensity when she sucks my bottom lip into her mouth. Her suck is warm and soft and pillowy, just like her mouth feels around my dick. The timer goes off, and she finishes with a sweet, parting kiss.

"Your turn," she says, as if we were playing chess.

I roll the dice and end up with blow on, bellybutton, and five minutes. "Seriously?" I ask. "I'm rolling again, because blowing on your bellybutton for five minutes is not my idea of sexy, and you happen to have a lot of parts I want to get at." My indignant response is funny to her, but I'm still rolling again.

This time I roll, one minute, suck, and nipple. "Now that's more like it," I say with a devious grin. I pin her down on the floor while I crawl up her body. The fact that her nipples are so apparent through the lace makes me give in to my earlier desire to suck them through the sheer material and leave the lace cold and wet for the duration of the game. A minute goes by in a flash, but after the timer goes off, I still manage to nudge the wispy fabric to the side with my nose and get a few tongue swipes against her bare nipple.

"Is it hot in here?" she asks as she sits up.

"Yeah, Baby it's really fuckin hot in here," I say with bawdy confidence, then drop the dice in her hand, "Roll."

She looks down at the dice, then announces, "Tug on, ten seconds, and clitoris, but since you don't happen to have a clitoris, I get to choose what I tug on for ten seconds," she smiles as she takes my hands and directs me to sit up on my knees.

"Ok, as long as it's my dick," I say, and I'm not even sure I'm kidding.

"Don't start the timer until I start tugging," she says, as if I wouldn't allow her the entire allotted time. Shit, I may set it for ten minutes.

She's facing me, and we are both on our knees when she slides her hands inside the back of my jeans, over my commando ass. When she starts pushing my jeans down, my cock flings free and sways heavily with the liberty. She shoves my jeans down my thighs and slowly drags the palms of her hands up the fronts of my legs. She is toying with me, but she hasn't even grazed my cock yet. Then she reaches down and grabs my balls.

I suck in a hasty breath and lock eyes with her. She cups my package for a few seconds, lightly jostling my nuts until she tightens her grip firmly around the top of my sack, so my balls are held snugly in the taut skin of my scrotum. She leans forward and whispers, "Start the timer, Salinger."

I set it as well as I can under the circumstances. What she's doing doesn't hurt exactly, but it threatens to, and considering how fragile the jewels are, I'm surprised I haven't even flinched. The sensation feels like a dull thrumming, like my balls have their own heartbeat, but at the same time, there is a tremendous need to satiate the urge to bury my cock in her. When the timer goes off, it's with relief as well as confounding disappointment that she releases the tug.

I'm sweating now, and it's not from the fireplace next to us. I think it's from pure, unadulterated *restraint*. I stand, then regretfully tuck the fellas back down into my jeans. When I finish, she drops the dice into my palm then sits back, very seductively with her knees open. I can't wait to pound her into the floorboards tonight.

I toss the dice onto the blanket between her open, teasing legs. We both laugh at the result—spank, ten minutes, earlobe.

"I'm not spanking your earlobe," I say with a self-righteous smirk. This will be fun, plus she has the perfect outfit on for getting spanked because the skirt doesn't cover her ass when she's *standing*, let alone when I bend her over. I'm starting to change my mind about this game, maybe it's not so ridiculous after all.

I get up so I can sit on the front arm of the couch, then I tap my lap while grinning like a hyena. "Come over here, you naughty little cock-tease, I have something for you."

She doesn't look a bit worried, but she should be because now it's my turn to tease, and I won't be merciful, not anymore. She leans over my lap, which is a perfect height with me sitting on the wide arm of the couch. She's still wearing heels so when she bends over, her legs are straight, and her ass is angled up in pouty perfection. When she rests her hands on the couch cushion for support, her upper body is raised from my lap a bit. That suits me just fine because first I unclasp her top, then watch it peel away from her flawless breasts to drop on the seat of the couch.

I rub my hand all over her bare ass and then skim my palm under her G-string, pulling it away from her body. When I lower the scrap of panties down her thighs, I can feel her shiver. Then I resume caressing her naked ass while she slips one foot out of the thong that's pooled around her ankles.

"Spread your legs," I demand, as my fingers graze over and between her silky lips.

199

The first smack comes without warning, I can feel it prickling on my palm as her ass simultaneously heats up.

"Mmmmmm, do it again," she says with a plea in her voice.

Smack!

She lowers her chest even more, then waves her booty while it's poised in the air. Perhaps I've met my match with her. I love all the kinky stuff, but I prefer to keep it within a relationship instead of dipping into the club to satisfy the proclivity. She seems to agree and has risen to each occasion, even surpassing my expectations. I like that she has a little freak in her. It's going to be fun drawing it out. Not to mention, it will for sure keep things fresh in the bedroom.

Smack!

Smack!

There is a certain numbness in my hand that I'm sure goes double for her, but she doesn't seem to mind. I love how each time I spank her, her ass jiggles from the force, it's the sexiest ripple I've ever seen run through someone's body. She groans with pleasure. Obviously, she likes being spanked.

I only have ten minutes, and I want to offer some variety, so this time instead of the expected ass smack, I briskly tap her pussy. She writhes against me, so I do it again. Her moaning is exciting the fuck out of me, but she's in more of a drowsy trance—that simply won't do. I slide my fingers through her wetness until I find her clit. At first, I only apply pressure to it, but gradually I work little circles against her.

After a while of alternating sharp spanks with gentle little orbits around her clit, she no longer is holding her head up. Instead, she lets it fall forward in a resigned display of surrender.

When I look over and notice that she forgot to set the timer, I smile to myself then ease my finger inside her with sinful satisfaction. Clearly, her spanking has veered off course, but as far as I'm concerned, we are finished with the game.

Chapter Thirty One

New Year's

After Avery comes all over my fingers, I help her stand up next to me. Then I circle her nipples with my wet fingers. I don't even need to blow on them to get them to tighten further, but I do. Then I suck first one and then the other into my mouth, tasting her and groaning with rapidly decreasing patience.

She slides off her shoes while I passionately step out of my jeans then we reconvene on the rumpled blankets in front of the fire. I catch a glimpse of my watch and stop kissing her rather abruptly.

"Oh, shit!" I say. "I mean, Happy New Year!" I'm laughing at the fact that we missed the ball drop by more than twenty minutes, but she doesn't seem to mind.

"It's all good, my New Year's resolution already came to fruition," she says with a grin.

"And hardly half an hour into the New Year," I tease. "What was it, to up your cardio with multiple jaw clenching orgasms?"

"Nope. It was to seduce you and get the sexy, unattainable, Salinger Davis into my bed."

"I'm not terribly sure you should be so cocky about that, I haven't been in your bed yet," I say while pointing out the glaring technicality. The truth is, I have never actually fucked her in her bed. "You should keep trying though, because I've decided to be quite attainable for my New Year's resolution," I smile.

"Ok then, I'll keep trying," she says wickedly, "Looks like I'm going to have to up my game."

"Yes, see that you do."

We kiss for a bit in front of the crackling fire, our bodies naked and comfortably entwined before she says, "Can you get the champagne? We need to toast to the New Year."

I tear myself away from her warm body, then follow my cock into the kitchen to get two glasses and the Champagne from the fridge. When I come back, Avery has moved one of the blankets partially onto the couch and is sitting on her heels on the floor next to it.

I hand her both glasses, which really are just small mason jars like your grandma used when she made homemade jam, but because the cabin lacks Champagne flutes, they will have to do. I pop the cork without letting any pressure build up, so the surge is minimal. After I pour some into both glasses and put the bottle down on the end table, Avery hands me one of them.

"Cheers," she says with a bare naked smile.

"Yeah, Happy New Year," I smile back, then take a sip. The truth is, I dislike Champagne, it's too sweet and too fizzy. However, we did just turn the page on a new chapter, and I don't only mean the New Year, so I will enjoy this bubbly sweetness to the fullest.

"Sit here," she motions to the blanketed section of the couch. "And lean way back."

I do as I'm told, hoping this scenario ends with my dick in her mouth. It looks promising as Avery rises to her knees and settles herself between my legs. She takes ahold of my unwieldy boner with one hand, then with the other, she pours some of her chilled champagne on my package. The temperature startles me, as does the fizzing, but nothing prepares me for when she leans forward and licks it off my sack. Fuck that feels so good. Then she pours another light trickle on me as she sucks a ball into her mouth.

I can feel my eyes roll back in my head. The sensation is crazy, it's cold, it's bubbly, and then her hot mouth.....Fucking hell!

She backs off with a slurp to reach for the bottle and pour more Champagne into her glass. She's not shy with the pour because she fills it all the way to the rim of the mason jar. My nuts are bursting full and quaking with the need to unload, and she's trickling more bubbles on me and then licking a ball into her mouth, and, oh fuuuuck it's good! She is gentle with my fragile testicles while still being assertive, and I am not-going-to-last.

"Aves, I need a condom right now," I say with my own assertiveness.

"Hmmmmmmmm?" she hums against my nut, and I almost lose it. She pulls back again, "I won't get pregnant, I want you bare."

Those words are enough for me to spring forward, and turn her around as I adjust my knees on the floor blankets. Now she is sitting on my lap, reverse cowgirl with her shins against the blankets by each of mine, and my cock is against her ass crack pointing north. I press her forward, so she has to support herself with her hands and widen her knees. I have a grip on her hips with both hands, and within a second or two I have guided my cock deep into her warm grip.

I need to be still for a second, just to compose myself. The feel of her against my bare cock is intense, and I'm still not at all used to condom-less sex. She must realize I'm in a holding pattern that mimics purgatory because she holds still as well. Until she doesn't.

Then my hands tighten on her hips and start to rock her forward and back, my cock slipping easily in and out of her pussy. I want to do this all night, so I go nice and slow and am careful about my depth. The fire is settling down, but it still feels hot against the left side of my body as I guide Avery's hips forward and back, forward and back.

When she starts to groan against my depth, I realize I'm holding her so tightly against me, that on her backslide, her ass presses into my stomach. My advance has become intense and sonorous, and I am seriously close to coming. So, I release one hip and reach around, sliding my hand down her stomach and finding her clit. There is no time to waste, so I rub her fast and hard against my grinding depth until she starts to chant, "Oh, yes. Ohhh, yes. Ohhh, yes," and then, "Salinger! I'm com…ing!"

She doesn't even need to announce it because I can feel every convulsing pulse from the walls of her pussy with shocking clarity. Then my own release barrels down on me with the force of an imploding star. I can't even quantify how much cum I pump into her because it's so much. It's already oozing out around my still-engaged cock, as I slide a few more strokes into her.

We are both so wiped out, I hardly get my glasses on the end table before we both flop down on our makeshift bed. She cuddles against me while I drag the blanket from the couch to cover us. I'm enough of a gentleman to make sure the wet, Champagne spot is on top of me and not her, but I'm not sure she would care.

We are clamped tightly together when she whispers, "Goodnight, Salinger," and it is the most angelic sound I have ever heard, I want to hear it every night for the rest of my life.

"Goodnight, my sweet Avery."

Chapter Thirty Two

Cold

I wake up to Avery shivering and trying to wiggle under me in her sleep. It's cold as fuck because the fire has gone out. Nash has even made his way over to our feet in an attempt to glean some body heat from us. I try to ease out of the blankets without waking Avery up, but my movements are sudden and jerky due to the cold, and my current naked status.

It takes me three times as long to get the fire going because of my outright shivering but eventually it flickers to life. The immature flames make it seem like I'm trying to heat the room with a Bunsen burner, but I load up the logs anyway, hoping they too will catch the breath of the flame.

When I turn around Avery is holding the blanket open to me, and I all but dive in. She adheres herself to my frigid body, and I swallow her in my arms, desperate to warm up. I have to pee like a racehorse but can't force myself to get up again, not yet.

After a few minutes of being pressed against her head to toe nakedness, I warm up enough to make a break for the bathroom. However, I don't have any level of confidence that my pee stream will not freeze solid and fuse me to the process until the Spring thaw. If there is one thing I know for sure, it's that I'm not cut out for frontier living. I installed radiant heat coils under the tile in both of my bathrooms, so I don't need to walk across the polar ice caps just to take a piss. Would it have killed this guy to service his furnace once and awhile?

When I slide back into our cold, inhospitable bed, Avery places her thigh over my hip while she rubs her hand up and down my back, trying to warm me with the friction of it. Suddenly, all I am aware of is the proximity of her vagina to my dick. I close my eyes and try very hard to ignore it while I slowly rub her back as well.

The long, cold march to the bathroom was enough to wake me completely, but Avery is still cute and sleepy while trying to snuggle against some of the body heat I don't currently possess. The fire is still pretty bush league and has yet to roar to life, but the feel of Avery draped over me and pressed into my chest is all I need to stop shivering. After a while, her breathing slows, and I know she is sound asleep.

***

Over coffee and scrambled eggs on English muffins, I announce with authority, "I say we sleep in the bedroom tonight. If we close the door to the bunk bed room, we only have to heat that one room. There is a fireplace in there...we can sleep in a bed..."

"I thought you were worried about the pipes freezing?" Avery says over the rim of her coffee mug. Her hair is all disheveled, and I like the idea that I had a part in rumpling it up.

"I'm still worried about that, I will get a fire going out here right before we go to bed, and I'll get up to throw some more logs on it in the night. It doesn't need to be toasty warm, just warm enough for the pipes not to freeze." Then I lean in and say, "I want to be the reason your legs shake, not the bitter cold."

"Got it. Bedroom it is tonight," she says with a little bit of a shy smile on her face.

"As for today, I thought it would be fun to go rent snowmobiles."

"Really! I've never done that before," she gushes. It's so easy to put a smile on her face. I can't believe guys have not tripped all over themselves to do it.

It's supposed to be warmer today, and sunny, but that doesn't change the fact that there are several feet of snow on the ground.

"I brought two camelbacks we can fill with water, we'll pack some food, and then just take off and go explore the mountains."

"What about Nash?" she asks.

"He's all right, he can hold down the fort." I finish my coffee and look at her, all sexed up and tousled. How did I get so lucky? And why did I push her away for so long? "Come on, let's go get dressed," I finish, with the crack of emotion caught in my throat.

Chapter Thirty Three

Shower

When we get back from an entire day of snowmobiling—both of us sunburned across our noses where our sunglasses left off—Nash is good and pissed. He had visions of coming with us that were dashed as he watched us drive away from the cabin. He makes an urgent dash out the front door to go pee the moment Avery cracks it open, and then we both stand on the porch to watch him frolic in the snow after he relieves himself.

Avery leans into me, and I drape my arm over her shoulders. Is it weird that I am happy for the first time… in, perhaps my entire adult life? I can't remember feeling this light and optimistic ever, and the realization of such a thing is both desperately sad and wildly exciting.

"I'm going to cook for you tonight," she says as she loops both arms loosely around my waist. "But first, we both need to shower."

"Sounds good, because I'm hungry…and dirty," then my mouth is on hers.

***

I have worked the fire into a blazing inferno, hoping a morsel of heat will make its way into the Siberian climate of the bathroom. There is no telling if the hot water heater is up to the shower challenge because it probably shares a similar inception date as the furnace. That is, the furnace that crapped out in such a timely manner only days ago.

Avery puts a few bottles on the shower ledge, starts the water and bravely undresses, demonstrating her vote of confidence in having heated water. I watch her strip with greedy interest then notice the door of the shower start to steam up. Let's hope it lasts.

I undress and step in with her. She already has her hair lathered with shampoo that smells like sunshine and flowers. I soap up my palms then give her a hand with the rest of her shower.

After she is thoroughly clean and the water rinses down her body in sleek rivulets, she returns the favor. She too is quite meticulous while washing the ripeness off of me. While I'm still slippery with soap suds, I pull her into me. Our bodies are warm and slithery against each other. I could stand here and kiss her all night like this, but of course, the water starts to cool. We quickly rinse our bodies, then I turn off the water while she tugs two towels off the towel bar.

She wraps hers around herself, and I use mine to gently squeeze the trickling water from her hair, then dry myself off quickly and tie it around my waist.

"I want to wear something sexy for you, but it's too cold," she says, and I laugh.

"Aves, snow pants and a parka look sexy on you. Do you think warm clothes will detract from anything?" I mean that sincerely, she looked fucking hot this afternoon, and more than once I wanted to slide her snow pants down and take her on the back of my snowmobile.

She smiles, not sure if she should believe me or not. "Ok, at least let me dry my hair and put some makeup on."

I shrug, if it makes her feel better, fine. Then I swipe some deodorant on and brush my teeth again. As I'm walking out of the bathroom with the towel around my waist, I remember something, "Hey, we still haven't exchanged Christmas gifts yet."

"Oh, yeah. Let's do it at dinner," she says as she opens her towel just to adjust it, and my mouth falls open. It was just for a second, only a glimmer of a flash but the image is frozen to the backs of my eyelids.

She doesn't even realize what she did or how it affected me, but I'm looking very forward to giving her her present. Actually, I got her two, but they are both little. She made me promise that we would only exchange little token gifts, and I had agreed. So that's what they are, little token gifts that will keep on giving—just like the jelly of the month club.

***

Avery was able to create an amazing meal out of all the random food I brought. She made chicken breasts with a creamy, white wine and bacon sauce that she swears she just made up, but we will definitely be recreating it in the future. I made a decent salad with feta and candied walnuts to go along with the chicken, but it gets totally upstaged by Avery's culinary deliciousness.

When we finish eating, Avery wants to make some hot mulled wine, which is apparently a cold weather staple. All you need is red wine, bourbon and some spices that we may, or may not use from the stash in the cabinets. For example, the cinnamon sticks which could literally be thirty years old. Either way, stale cinnamon sticks or not, hot drinks by the fire sounds perfect, even if we do poison ourselves with old, colonial spices.

While Avery heats up the wine on the stove, I move all the floor blankets back to the bedroom and get the fireplace going in there, so the bed is not as cold as it was last time. Then I move the coffee table back into place between the couch and the hearth.

By the time I have everything picked up, and back to normal, Avery comes over with our mulled wine. It smells strong, and after one sip, I have confirmation that it is indeed a very stiff drink.

"Whewww, it's possible that I put too much bourbon in it," she says with a scrunched up face.

"Good, because I'm going to get you drunk and take advantage of you," I say. She can consider that her fair warning because all day I have thought about fucking her, and it's about time to see the daydream to fruition.

"Salinger?" Avery asks.

I look into her eyes, she sounds hesitant, so I'm extra interested in what she's about to say. "What?"

"Will you tell me about the girls at the club?" she looks away for a second, then back to my eyes. I know she is uncomfortable asking, but I am *hugely* uncomfortable answering.

"I'll tell you anything. What do you want to know about the girls at the club?" I need clarification, is she asking about the freaky stuff I've done with them, or how invested in them I was, or what they are like as people? I don't know the direction we are headed in, but I won't hide anything from her.

"Are they...like...more sexual than me?" she sounds insecure, and I don't recognize that emotion in her. I hope she doesn't think she is in competition with club girls because there is absolutely no comparison.

"Are they more sexual than you? No." I put both of our thousand-octane drinks down on the coffee table and take one of her hands between mine. "Some of them have some unusual kinks they are in to, but that doesn't make them more sexual, just different."

"But, am I boring to you after you've been with them?"

My eyes nearly bug out of my head, "Boring? Are you kidding me? The very *last* thing I am when I'm with you is bored."

"Do those girls give you something you can't get from me?" She is trying hard to keep looking me in the eyes, I can tell she wants to remain strong, but jealousy is unfamiliar to her. It suddenly dawns on me that she thinks I'm still planning on going to the club. Now that I realize that, I'm glad to be having this conversation.

"Yeah, they do." I feel her deflate before I go on. "They give me detachment. They give me hollow emotions. Avery, the most they ever did was fill an impersonal space of apathy for me."

Her eyes start to well up with tears that she quickly blinks away.

"Aves, those women were a distraction for me at a time when I needed to be distracted."

"You never cared for any of them?" she asks.

I think about how emotionally broken Bradley is and about Mary-Jane's issues with her ex, and I realize that I do care for them. I care about them in the way that I want good things for them. I want to see them land on their feet, but do I care about having them in my life? No, I don't.

"The club caters to a very basic, physical component. It doesn't nurture lasting relationships or even a sense of real connection."

"You didn't answer my question. Do you have feelings for any of those women?"

"Avery, I wish them well, and I want them to be happy. So in that way, yes, I care about them."

She nods but doesn't say anything. I can almost feel the lump in her throat in my own. I have to ease her mind, I'm in love with her, and I don't care if I see the girls from the club ever again. Yes, I said it. I'm in love with her. I am, but this is hardly the conversation I want to introduce those words to.

"Avery, the club filled a very shallow hole for me, but I need something deeper, more meaningful, and *you* fill *that* hole for me."

"Will you still want to go?"

"Absolutely not. I don't miss a single thing about the club," I say with conviction, then add, "There is nothing there for me. Do you know why?"

She slowly shakes her head.

"Because everything I need, is right here."

She lets out a choked breath then leans forward into my embrace. I hold her for a while, with her face pressed against the hollow of my neck, then I slide her into my lap. I had been sitting with one knee toward her so I could face her better, which makes for an awkward transition, but we both need this. I can hear her breath catch before she pauses and then tries to speak again.

"I've been so worried you wouldn't want to give it up, and it would kill me to have to share you."

I close my eyes against my own emotion before I respond. "I promise you, on my honor, you will *never* have to share me with another woman…unless we make girl babies, then it's going to be tough for me."

She laughs, and I can feel the tension drain from her body.

"Now hand me that drink, I still need to get you drunk so I can have my way with you."

Chapter Thirty Four

Gifts

Both Avery and I are on our second mulled wine cocktail, and I can already feel my lips going a little numb. For the most part, I can hold my liquor. Avery, on the other hand, is making me laugh at how animated and giggly she gets when she has a little too much to drink. I wouldn't call her a lightweight exactly, but mixing wine with a healthy amount of good old-fashioned Kentucky bourbon is maybe a bit much for her. Despite what I said earlier, the last thing I want to do is take advantage of a drunk Avery.

It's time to give her her Christmas gifts, so on my way to retrieve them I swing by the kitchen and get her a bottle of water from the fridge. On second thought, I grab one for me too.

We reconvene back on the couch before she reiterates, "It's just a token gift, right?" Our relationship advanced to the next level only a couple days before Christmas, and with something so new, we weren't sure what to do. Neither of us wanted to do *nothing*, but a sentimental gift would have been too much so soon. Therefore, we landed on getting each other *a little something*. So, here we are.

"You have two?" she asks when she sees both boxes.

"Why don't you open them before you get too worked up," I say, because neither one is much of anything.

She starts with the first one and lights up as she pulls it from the tissue paper. It happens to be very sexy, red crotch-less panties...with a twist. Though they are technically crotch-less, they have a row of pearls toward the front, and evidently, do quite a service when worn.

"Should I put them on?" she asks, though I'm sure she already knows the answer to that. She steps out of her sweatpants, and I suck in my breath when I see she isn't wearing any panties. Had I known this, I would have been very distracted while making and eating dinner. Commando in sweatpants is almost as hot as red, pearl string panties.

When she puts them on she says coyly, "Can you help me adjust them?"

My penis is already filling with blood , and my balls are gearing up for a party, but yes, I can absolutely adjust a string of pearls against her slit. She takes a step forward then pulls off her sweatshirt, so it doesn't get in my way. What *does* get in my way is the sight of her braless tits under a tight, white, long-underwear shirt. I can't look away, her areolas are completely visible, and her nipples are hard.

She steps closer, between my legs where I'm frozen to the couch. I place my hands on her ass and ever so slowly stroke her bare skin before dragging my palms down the backs of her thighs. I feel like I have sensory overload, the sight of her boobs, the feel of her skin, knowing the pearls are right in front of me on her mostly naked pussy, just waiting for me to spread her lips apart and align the pearls up against her clit. Oh, fuck. She's sexy.

I swallow hard and tear my eyes from her nipples, only to have them land on the crotch-less part of the panties. She purposely hasn't slid the panties all the way up, so the five, round pearls have not yet engaged with her provocative stance.

I coax the sides of the panties higher, closer to her hips, which finally brings the pearls in contact with her slit. I reach over and tease her lips apart with two fingers, then lean forward and lick straight up her crease. She gasps because she wasn't expecting it, but now the pearls can slide easily between her licked pussy lips and press wickedly against her clitoris.

"What now?" she laments.

"Now you have a seat and open the next one," I say, knowing the pearls will press against her when she sits. Which they do, if the look on her face is any indication. She unwraps the next gift and slowly starts to pull out one end of a silk scarf. She looks like a magician the way she keeps pulling, and the scarf keeps coming.

"Is this so you can tie me up?" she asks with a smile, "Or blindfold me?"

"We can do both of those too," I raise my eyebrows at her, impressed with her imagination. "But there's this cool trick I want to try where I tie it around my cock and balls, leaving a knot on top so it can rub against your pretty clit while you ride me."

"Oh," she says. She is flustered, the pearls pressing against her and the talk of riding me with a knot against her clit is really making her heart pound, I can see it plainly on her face.

"Your turn," she says as she hands me a gift bag brimming with tissue paper.

I pull out a tiny, sheer black outfit with lace ruffles at the bottom. I can feel the back of my neck heat up because this is going to be very tight and very see-through. There is a little scrap of G-string that goes with it, but it's hardly worth mentioning.

"Do you like it?" she asks, but I'm pretty sure the fact that I'm almost drooling answers her question.

"I don't know yet. Maybe I should see it on," I look up, but refrain from jumping on her, which takes every little bit of restraint I possess. "Come over here, I'll help you," I say, and it sounds predatory, dangerous in fact.

She moves slowly, carefully adjusting herself on my lap, facing me. When she leans forward to raise the hem of my long-underwear shirt, her breath catches. It's barely audible, but it reminds me of the vulnerable state of her excitement. The pearls appear rather incessant, and with her legs spread above my lap, it's obvious they are nudging against her. I let her help with the removal of my shirt, but I'm not done enjoying how her tits look in hers. The tiny, waffle texture of the tight shirt across her highly visible nipples draws both my hands and my mouth to them.

I start with bumping my thumbs roughly over her nipples and then transition to scratching my fingernails across them. They are highly responsive to my indelicate approach, so I lean forward and nip one with my teeth while pinching the other. I suck one and then the other. Then, once the white fabric is damp over each nipple, I lean back to revel in the raunchiness of the sight.

My hands are already on her thighs, so I move my thumb to gently flutter the pearls against her. My eyes are still ensnared by her wet, straining nipples, but the effect of my ministrations below are quite obvious. She rocks her head back, which only presses her tits forward to further hypnotize me. Then she starts to croon.

I had intended on undressing her so she could put on the sheer black outfit, but there has been a change of plans. I hold her against me then stand up from the couch. After she wraps her legs around me, I carry her to the bedroom with my mouth against the side of her throat, kissing and breathing my need in hot, heavy breaths.

Though it's plenty warm in here with the fire going, I still peel back the blankets before I lay her down on the bed. I yank the buttons of my fly open and roughly climb out of my jeans. My boner feels like it has weights attached to it, it's so heavy and ponderous.

Once I peel off Avery's shirt, she pulls the blankets over the top of us. Before we are even fully covered, I've pressed into her with what could be considered reckless abandon, except that it's still so tender and sweet.

This is the sex I prefer, not the kinky, dirty club sex, this. This connection is so important to me. The physicality is amazing, but fireworks sex is nothing without this connection. We are kissing and clinging to the rawness of the act, as our nakedness fuses us together. I can feel the string of pearls to the side, as I slide tightly in and out of her. It creates a hard sensation against the side of my cock that runs in stark contrast to the velvety feel of Avery all over me.

I pull slightly away from our kiss and whisper, "Avery, I love you."

She moves her hands from my back so she can circle my neck with her arms. Then she pulls me more tightly against her, and with her lips next to my ear, she says, "I love you too, Salinger. So much," and then she is sniffling and crying against my cheek, and the whole thing is so fucking tender, it's downright poetic.

Chapter Thirty Five

Morning

I wake up to Avery kissing my back. Actually, she is kissing my scar. The skin feels warm like it's a part of me in a way it hasn't been since before the explosion. I can already feel my erection pressing into the mattress when she says, "Good morning."

I slowly roll over, but my grogginess vaporizes when I see her sitting on the bed, naked except for the silk scarf tied around her tits like a belted sash.

"I've already started coffee, let Nash out, and put more logs on both fires. I had to restart the one in the living room, but it's raging now."

"You look beautiful. I could really get used to this disheveled, well-fucked look of yours," I smile as I bring both wrists behind my head. I'm interested to see where this goes.

"I was hoping to add *well fucked* to this morning's routine," she says with a sideways smile that looks a little devilish if you want to know the truth.

"You are insatiable."

"Looks like you are too," she says with a nod to the sheet tent above my salute. "And after you fuck me, I want to go down to the horseback riding stables we saw yesterday and rent some horses."

"Should I brush my teeth first?" I ask as I reach for my glasses on the nightstand. I don't want to miss any of this to blurry vision.

"I didn't," she says as she slowly pulls one end of the bow that's tied across her chest. It unties all at once and drops to her lap. "Tell me if I'm doing this right," she says, as she pulls the sheet off my huge, morning wood.

She wraps the scarf around the base of my balls and ties it above my cock. Then she tips her head to the side as if contemplating something. I like that she is studying my dick so closely. It's completely erect and proud right now, it's not even a little shy about her close scrutiny. Then she unties the scarf and starts again. This time, she folds the length of it in half before repeating the previous process.

"Is it too tight?" she asks.

"No," I answer. Honestly, it had been too tight at first, but the silk must have relaxed a bit because now it's snug but not uncomfortable. It should work like a cock ring to restrict the blood flow out of my cock and keep me as rigid as a slab of granite.

She climbs on, straddling my body before she grabs my cock and guides it in, very, very slowly. I can feel her squeezing against me, and I have to close my eyes because the sensation and the view of her above me are almost too much. The lust is clouding my brain and flushing me with massive amounts of dopamine. Fuck, it's so good.

"I don't want to feel the knot just yet, I'm afraid that much direct stimulation will make me come too soon," she says, mirroring my exact thoughts about how bare sex feels for me. Then she surprises me by turning her body and pulling one of my knees up, so my leg is bent. She moves so that one of her knees is on the bed between my legs and she is grinding against my hip and thigh. It's a type of cowgirl position except that she is riding me sideways, pressing against my bent leg instead of my pelvis. Seeing her sideways like this, grinding against me, fucking me—is new for me. This position is altogether new to me, but it's fantastic. I can see the arch to her back and the way she moves, holy shit.

"Aaaaaa, Salinger! This is so good. I want to fuck you like this forever."

It *is* so good, and she looks damn hot in control like this. I don't think I will ever get enough of her. My mind is fucking blown.

By the time she adjusts her legs and slides me back inside her, so she can rock against the knot, I'm thanking God for the scarf around my goods. I think I would have erupted ten minutes ago without it. Her tits are in my face, and my hands are on her ass, and all I can think about is how perfect everything is.

Her orgasm goes off like tiny jolts against my cock. Her body sparks and she groans as it rumbles through her. Normally, I would let go and come with her, but the silk around my package delays that too. She flops down on my chest panting, which is when my orgasm finally squeezes me in its fist. I clench my eyes and jaw and unload into her as I hug her tightly to my body.

We both lie here in reflective silence. I think well-deserved happiness is figuratively drifting down on us like snowflakes. The snow doesn't understand the metaphor, and the flakes don't know their role as tiny bits of happiness, but still, when they land, they seep into our skin and become part of us. I think we have both waited a long time for the other, but sometimes life needs to teach us something about ourselves before deeming us ready for the next rung of the ladder.

I'm grateful to take that step with Avery, and I look forward to all the rungs that follow. She is a part of me now. I will always relish being with her, and I will crave her when we're apart. When I say, *crave her*, it's not just her body I'll crave, it's her soul.

I want all of her. The broken down, the insecure, the crushing passion that comes with her job, the starry-eyed wonderment she brings to each new experience—everything that makes her, her. I never want to spend another day without her. I need her with me like I've never needed another human being.

I feel like I've been subconsciously waiting for her, so I can finally rise from my ashes and become the Phoenix represented on my arm. The Phoenix, and the man I deserve to be.

Chapter Thirty Six

Epilogue

Jessie is about a month away from giving birth to Corey and Devin's daughter, Evelyn Grace. Both daddies chose the name Evelyn, and Jessie chose Grace. She could not be more excited to be done with being pregnant. It's not that she hasn't enjoyed the tiny flutters that evolved into impatient kicks and stretches, or the excitement of doctor's appointments and ultrasound pictures, it's that she's anxious to get back into shape and start planning her wedding.

For all my original disdain for Silas, I have to admit he has turned out to be a great guy. In fact, the whole rag-tag bunch of us is more like family to each other now instead of the disjointed friendships here and there we started with.

Ruby calls Avery and me, *Auntie* and *Uncle*, and I'm sure the new baby will too. Corey and Devin's house is finally finished, and it is exactly how you would picture Devin's house to be—highly designed and a bit over the top.

There was a big push to finish before the baby gets here which led to some hilarious banter and a few sulky fights between the two of them, but they are so well suited for each other, it barely caused a hick-up between them.

With the house finished, Jessie will be moving in with Silas and renting out her condo. She has offered it to Avery, but I have other plans.

"Are you ready, Hon?" Avery asks. She is standing next to me in her baby shower dress that I want to unzip and leave crumpled on the floor. She is holding a giant gift bag full of pink tissue paper.

"Yep, let me just grab my keys," I say as I turn on my heel. When I come back, I have a smaller gift bag that I hand to Avery as I take the baby's gift from her.

"What is this?" she asks.

"It's just a little something for you," I say with a fat smile on my face.

She reaches into the bag and pulls out a keychain with a single key on it. When she looks back up into my eyes, she is smiling too.

"Does this mean I won't be renting Jessie's condo when my lease is up next month?"

I nod. "Unless you don't like that key, in which case we can go looking for another set of keys."

"Salinger, I would love to move in with you." She steps into me for a pretty solid kiss for two people who are supposed to be at a baby shower. "But you will need to clean out the garage so I can park in there too."

I smile against her mouth. I'll do that and a whole lot more if it means falling asleep with her every night and waking up with her every morning. I'm not in a big hurry to get married again but I *will* marry Avery one day, and we will have baby showers of our own.

The End

Keep Reading for a Sneak Peek at Little Dove, KC's Gritty New Standalone

Also by KC Decker:
LITTLE DOVE
OF ASH AND ANGELS

To My Fans:

From the bottom of my heart, I want to thank you for taking this journey with me. It wasn't always pretty (trust me on that) but I hope it was worth it, and I hope I've earned your approval.

It means the world to me that you gave me a shot as a new author, and rode this series all the way to shore.

I am honored to interact with each of you through social media, and I'm always open for questions or general comments. I strive very hard to respond personally to each one of you, because you've all played a role in the success of my books. For that commitment to me, and your undying support, I wish you all, happiness beyond measure.

Love,

—KC

JOIN KC DECKER:

Mailing List: www.KCDeckerBooks.com
Instagram: www.instagram.com/author_kc_decker
Twitter: www.twitter.com/KCDeckerBooks
Facebook: www.facebook.com/kc.decker.79
Bookbub: www.bookbub.com/profile/kc-decker

www.KCDeckerBooks.com

If you would like to be added to my Street Team of Kick-Ass Reviewers and Bloggers, email me at KCDecker@camden-publishing.com

Little Dove Available Now!

Bonus Material
Little Dove

Chapter One

Thinking

My name is Etta Freeman. That's what it will say on my gravestone anyway, not that many will come to my funeral. I'm sure my death will make the five o'clock news, horrific as it was, and everyone will take a minute to feel sorry for my family and to be grateful it's not their daughter's weathered corpse found off highway forty-four. I say weathered because it will, no doubt, be some time before an unsuspecting hiker and their dog will stumble across my partially decomposed body.

I always suspected I would die this way, if not by his hands, then by another's. I knew if I dabbled in the dark some of it would seep into my skin. I knew it would take hold of my inherent goodness and smear it around the rest-stop floor. I should never have taken him on. I should have known his bad was much stronger than my good, that darkness has a way of snuffing out the light. Ask anyone who has ever seen a kid's patchy, bald head from chemotherapy or someone whose loved ones were pulled from beneath a drunk driver's car.

Certainly, there are disastrous outcomes in the form of accidents or circumstances that can't be avoided, but there are also evil people in the world that can't be fixed. They can't be rehabilitated and then thrust back into polite society. They fit in, but they don't belong, not any more than songbirds on the ocean floor. The individuals I'm referring to thrive on other people's pain and suffering, they seek only to cause harm and spread despair. I used to think they could be stopped. I wanted to help because I thought I could make a difference in the evil vacuum of purposeful wickedness. I couldn't help though. I didn't know how badly the darkness would fester around me. How it would cling to my body, suck out my light, and then drag me under the sludge in its mighty death-roll.

The darkness standing over me right now is just a man. He had to have been loved by someone at some point in his thirty or so years, but no love or light has penetrated his evil haze. He stinks of something sinister, but no one else can smell his rot. He is a terrible man. I call people like him *dark souls* even though they are as human as you or I. There is no level they won't sink to in order to sprinkle chaos and suffering around them like bird seed.

He must think I'm dead because he loosens his grip around my throat and disengages his vengeful penis from my torn and battered rectum. The blood and semen run warm from my body but quickly cool in the frigid night air. He went to great lengths and expended a tremendous amount of energy to rip through all parts of my body and pump me full of his evil seed. Now it can seep out from all the cuts on my body and be absorbed by the ground where it can fester and grow more despair.

Before climbing from the ditch, he steps on the back of my neck to further grind my teeth and face into the fallen leaves and muck. He's probably trying to break my neck or otherwise damage me for not slackening his malignant urges. Nothing will rid him of those. They are a part of him just like the prominent chin and his receding hairline. The malice that spills from him will never be enough to quench his dusty thirst. He will always seek to destroy the good in people.

In his final act of degradation, he kicks a boot full of dirt and filth over me as he spits on my lifeless body. He leaves me like this, mostly nude, with a mouthful of dirt and rotting leaves. My eyes have long since swollen shut, and the metallic tang of blood will be the last thing I taste.

I lie here, dead or dying and wonder why I feel so at peace. I would say I am already dead, except that I'm shivering from the cold leaves plastered intermittently to my body and the chill of urine that soaked me when my bladder let go.

Being strangled is a dubious process, there is the urine, sure, but it's also the straining of your eyes. The way they reach out of your body and try to slip from between the swollen lids. Your lips fill with blood too, as your face purples, they feel like they will split open and burst like two overcooked bratwursts. The dizziness is notable too, but maybe it's not as efficient to strangle someone from behind, because for me it was more like bouts of dizziness instead of overall, and I don't think I ever fully lost consciousness, not while he tried to choke me anyway.

Death can't be far off though, humans were not made to suffer this kind of brutality without reaching out toward the sanctity of beyond, extended arms straining for relief and the promise of solace. I feel like all I need to do is close my eyes to shed this world. Close them and step into the light, the light that has become familiar to me now. The light I have seen before.

End of Chapter 1
Little Dove

Thank you for reading! If you enjoyed 1700 Grant Street, PLEASE consider leaving a review...It would mean the world to me.

Love,
KC

CPSIA information can be obtained
at www.ICGtesting.com
Printed in the USA
LVHW090113050121
675744LV00022B/74